"Do me a favor?"

"I'd do anything for you."

In that instant, she believed he meant those words. Her heart ached. "Kiss me."

There was just enough room between those bars. He could kiss her once more. It would be a kiss goodbye.

Sullivan instantly leaned toward her. His lips brushed against hers, and then that kiss deepened.

She hated the bars. If only she could touch him fully. Savor him.

Why had fate been working against them from the very beginning?

She gave herself fully to that kiss, trying to forget everything else in that moment but him. She'd always loved his taste. Loved the way his lips pressed to hers. Her heart galloped in her chest and she pressed ever closer to him.

She'd never wanted anyone more.

ALLEGIANCES

New York Times Bestselling Author
CYNTHIA EDEN

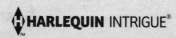

HARLEQUIN INTRIGUE®

Thank you, Denise Zaza and Shannon Barr!
It is truly a pleasure to work with you two wonderful ladies.

Recycling programs
for this product may
not exist in your area.

ISBN-13: 978-0-373-69903-2

Allegiances

Printed in U.S.A.

Cynthia Eden, a *New York Times* bestselling author, writes tales of romantic suspense and paranormal romance. Her books have received starred reviews from *Publishers Weekly*, and she has received a RITA® Award nomination for best romantic suspense novel. Cynthia lives in the Deep South, loves horror movies and has an addiction to chocolate. More information about Cynthia may be found at cynthiaeden.com, or you can follow her on Twitter, @cynthiaeden.

Books by Cynthia Eden

Harlequin Intrigue

The Battling McGuire Boys

Confessions
Secrets
Suspicions
Reckonings
Deceptions
Allegiances

Shadow Agents

Alpha One
Guardian Ranger
Sharpshooter
Glitter and Gunfire

Shadow Agents: Guts and Glory

Undercover Captor
The Girl Next Door
Evidence of Passion
Way of the Shadows

Visit the Author Profile page at Harlequin.com for more titles.

CAST OF CHARACTERS

Sullivan McGuire—Secrets have been Sullivan's life for as long as he can remember. Secrets...and danger. But he's tired of letting those secrets control him, and he is more than ready to fight for the one woman he has never been able to forget: Celia James.

Celia James—She isn't a delicate damsel in distress—she never has been. Celia is ex-CIA, and she is a woman who knows how to handle any challenge that comes her way. But when new danger stalks her *and* her former lover, Sullivan, Celia knows that she will risk anything in order to protect the only man she has ever loved.

Mac McGuire—Mac knows all about the nightmare from Sullivan's past. After all, he was there when his brother was rescued from his nightmarish prison, and he watched Sullivan try to put the pieces of his life back together. The one piece that was always missing from that life? Celia.

Ronald Worth—Celia's former supervisor at the CIA, Ronald is a man who understands danger and sacrifice. He knows where every skeleton is buried, and he was the man who helped Celia at some of her darkest times. But is he a man who can truly be trusted? Or is he working his own agenda?

Ben Howard—The police captain is in way over his head, and he knows it. Dealing with spies and CIA operatives is not part of his usual routine. He's sworn to uphold the law, and he wants to help Sullivan McGuire—after all, he owes that whole family—but paying them back with his *life* was never part of the deal.

Chapter One

"Hello, Sullivan."

At that low, husky voice—a voice Sullivan had heard far too many times in his dreams—his head whipped up. He blinked, sure that he had to be imagining the figure standing in his office doorway. He even shook his head, as if that small movement could somehow make the woman before him vanish.

Only she didn't vanish.

She laughed, and the small movement made her short red hair brush lightly against her delicate jaw. "No, sorry, you can't blink or even wish me away. I'm here." Celia James stepped inside and shut the door behind her.

He rose to his feet in a quick rush. "I wouldn't wish you away." Just the opposite. His voice had sounded too gruff, so he cleared his throat. He didn't want to scare her away, not when he had such plans for her. *And she's actually here. Close enough to touch.* "Should you... should you be here? You were hurt—"

Celia waved that injury away with a flick of her hand. "A flesh wound. I've had worse." Sadness flickered in her eyes. "It's Elizabeth who took the direct hit. I was afraid for a while...but I heard she's better now."

He nodded and crept closer to her. Elizabeth Snow

was the woman his brother Mac—MacKenzie—intended to marry as fast as humanly possible. Elizabeth was also the woman who'd been shot recently—when she faced off against a killer who'd been determined to put Elizabeth in the ground.

Only Elizabeth hadn't died, and in that particular case…it had brought Celia back into Sullivan's life.

Now I can't let her leave.

He schooled his expression as he said, "She's out at the ranch. And I'm sure Mac is about to drive her crazy." He was absolutely certain of that fact. His brother had broken apart when Elizabeth was shot. There was no denying the love Mac felt for her. "I think his protective instincts kicked into overdrive." *So did mine. When I saw you on the ground…*

Because Elizabeth hadn't been the only one hurt on that last case. Celia had also been caught in the cross fire.

But Celia didn't appear overly concerned with the injury she'd received. "I was knocked out for a few moments. My head hit the wall." Her calm expression dismissed the terrifying moment, but then, he knew it took a lot to terrify her. "The bullet just grazed me."

He hadn't realized that fact, not at first. He'd just known that she was limp in his arms.

A whole lot had sure come into crystal-clear perspective for him in those desperate moments.

"I came to make you a deal," Celia said as she took a step toward him.

His head tilted to the side as he studied her. "A deal?" Now he was curious. Celia wasn't exactly the type to make deals. She was the type to keep secrets. The type to always get the job done, no matter what.

During Sullivan's very brief stint with the CIA, he'd met the lovely Celia.

And he'd fallen hard for her.

Until I thought she'd betrayed me.

"I have information you want." She pulled a white envelope out of her purse. "I'll give it to you, but you have to promise me one favor."

Suspicious now, he asked, "And just what favor would that be?" She had plenty of government connections. She didn't need him now. Never had. He knew that now.

Her smile flashed. A smile that showed off her dimples. Those dimples were so innocently deceptive. So gorgeous.

So Celia.

They made her appear so delicate.

But the truth of the matter was…Celia James was a trained killer. One of the best to ever work for the CIA.

And she doesn't make deals.

Yet she was standing in his office, asking for one. The whole scene felt surreal to him.

"You have to agree *before* I tell you what I want." She shrugged. "Sorry, but it's one of those deal-in-the-dark situations. Promise me that you'll be there when I call in this debt. That you'll agree to what I need, and this information is yours." She waved the bulky envelope a bit, as if tempting him.

His gaze stayed locked on hers. He wanted to touch her. Needed to kiss her. Instead, he stood there and forced his body to be still. "Just what information is it that you *think* you have?" He didn't understand why Celia thought he'd be interested in any deal she had. He'd more than made it clear that he'd never work for the CIA again. He'd barely escaped before, when he'd been caught in a web of lies and death.

"I have your mother's real name." Her voice was soft, almost sympathetic.

But he wasn't impressed by her big reveal. He and his brothers had already uncovered his mother's real last name. They already knew—

"And I have the reason she was put in the Witness Protection Program."

Now, *that* information…he didn't know. And he was sure curious about why his mother had given up her previous life, adopted an entirely new name and wound up in Austin, Texas.

For years, Sullivan, his brothers and his sister had been working desperately to unmask the identity of the killers who had murdered their parents. One dark Texas night, two gunmen had broken into the McGuire ranch. They'd killed Sullivan's mother, then his father. Sullivan's sister, Ava, had managed to escape and get help, but that help hadn't arrived in time.

Years later, they were close—*finally* close—to unmasking the killers. They'd worked tirelessly on the case. When the local law enforcement authorities had given up the hunt, the family had formed a private agency, McGuire Securities. They'd kept working to solve a crime that would *never* be a cold case, not to them, and along the way they'd helped others with their investigation firm. McGuire Securities now had a top-notch reputation that drew in clients from the South and all along the East Coast.

Years ago, Sullivan had sworn he would never stop searching for the truth about that dark night, not until he'd given his parents the justice they deserved.

Celia offered the envelope to him. That white envelope looked so small and harmless in her hands, but it had the potential to change so much. "Do we have a deal?" Celia asked. "One favor, no questions asked… and you can have her past."

He stared at the envelope, and then he looked back up into Celia's blue eyes. "Deal." To learn more about his mother, he would have promised anything.

A faint sigh slipped from Celia's lips. She hurried toward him, closing the last of the distance between them.

His hand lifted and he took that envelope from her. Their fingers brushed, and the touch sent a hot, hard stab of need right through him. But that was the way it was for him when Celia was near. He saw her, he touched her and he just wanted. Some things couldn't be changed, no matter how much time passed.

"I'll be seeing you soon, Sully," she said as her fingers fell away from his. "And…good luck to you." Then she turned away and headed for the door.

That was it? She asked for a deal then just walked away? "Same old Celia," he murmured. "Secretive to the core, aren't you?" He put the envelope down on his desk.

She glanced back at him. Her red hair contrasted with her bright blue eyes—eyes that gave no hint to her emotions. "You know my life has to be about secrets."

Because she was an agent. CIA. Right. He got that. She was a real-life chameleon. When he'd known her before, her hair had been black. Her eyes…they'd been green. At first he'd thought he was seeing the real Celia back then. He hadn't known just how much of a mask she truly presented to the world. Then he'd gone to a team meeting a few days later, and she'd been blonde. With bright blue eyes.

The same eyes I see now.

She'd been able to change her appearance so quickly. She'd been able to *become* someone else with total ease, even adopting a new accent on command. She'd told him once that she could only be real with him.

With everyone else, she had an image to keep.

I should have believed her. But he hadn't. When the danger had closed in, he'd turned his back on her. "Would it matter," Sullivan asked her, aware that his voice had roughened, "if I told you that I was sorry?"

Something happened then. For just a moment, he saw a flash of emotion in her eyes.

Pain.

He hated that he'd hurt her. If he could, he'd take away any pain that she felt. He'd make sure she *never* felt pain again.

"Are you?" Celia asked him, cocking her head just a bit, as if it was now her turn to study him. "Are you sorry?"

He stared at her a moment, the past and present merging for him. He'd been drawn to Celia from the moment they first met. Without hesitation, he'd given in to his hunger for her. The passion had been hot, raging out of control, and when their world had imploded, he'd thought she'd been using him. Seducing him.

He hadn't realized—not until too late—that she'd loved him.

I lost her. "Yes," Sullivan said gruffly. "I am."

She smiled, and it was a smile that held bite. "Good. Then maybe when I come calling for that debt, you won't hesitate."

"I won't." He crossed the room and hurried to her side. He reached out to her.

But Celia put up her hand, stopping him. "Don't."

He wanted to touch her. Hold her. "Why can't we start again?" Did he sound desperate? Maybe. So what? When she'd been hurt on that last case, when she'd been lying so still on the ground, *everything* had changed for him. His priorities had shifted instantly.

Getting justice for his parents? Hell, yes, he would do that. He'd made a vow to himself, to his family, and he would keep it.

But getting Celia back in his life? Back in his bed? That was his immediate goal. Holding tightly to her and never letting go had become his obsession.

"We can't start again because you nearly destroyed me before," Celia said. "I needed you, and you left me."

He flinched at her soft words. Celia wasn't pulling any punches.

"But…" Celia shook her head. "You were always one fine marine, and you were incredible as a field agent."

Until he'd been taken. Because he'd been distracted…

By her. No, it hadn't been Celia's fault. None of it had been. Sullivan had been the one who wasn't on his game. He was the one who hadn't taken enough precautions. And he was the one who'd been afraid of what would come in the aftermath of his capture.

Even then, I didn't want her hurt. Even then, I was afraid of what could happen to her…because of me.

Her gaze was still on him. "I know that when you give your word," she added, "you mean it."

His hands fisted because the urge to reach out to her was too strong. He wanted to touch her. To see if her skin still felt like silk. Her scent—sweet, light—rose and wrapped around him.

"I'll see you again soon," she said. Then she opened the door. The heavy carpet swallowed her footsteps as she left him.

He stood there a moment, fighting the past and trying to figure out what the hell he should do in the present.

Go after her.

His head snapped up when he heard the ding of the elevator. And then Sullivan was racing down the hallway. The rest of McGuire Securities was deserted, so no one witnessed his frantic run. And it *was* frantic. But he couldn't just let her go, not like this. His hand flew out and he stopped the elevator, activating the sensors in the doors right before they closed.

Celia's eyes widened as she started. "Sullivan, what are you doing?"

What he should have done the first moment he looked up and saw her standing in his office.

"I gave you the envelope." She sounded dazed. "Have you even looked inside it?"

No, he'd left it on his desk, unopened. *Priorities.* He strode into the elevator.

She backed up against the wall. It was the first time he'd ever seen Celia retreat from anyone.

"I missed you," he gritted out.

Her lips parted.

"And you don't get to just vanish again."

Before she could respond, Sullivan leaned forward and he kissed her. His hands pushed against the elevator wall on either side of her head and he put his mouth on hers.

Her lips were still parted, just a bit, and his lips met

hers in a hot, openmouthed kiss. She tasted so sweet—even sweeter than he remembered—and Sullivan's heart drummed wildly in his ears. He held his body carefully away from hers, only touching her with his mouth. Touching her and trying like hell to seduce her with his lips and tongue. He kissed her a bit deeper, a bit harder, savoring her because it had been far too long since he'd been with her like this.

Far, far too long.

Dreams weren't enough for him. Memories weren't getting him through the long nights any longer. He needed her. Not a ghost. The real woman.

His Celia. But even as he deepened that kiss—

Her hands pressed to his chest and she shoved him back.

Sullivan's breath sawed out as he stared down at her.

"Do you like hurting me?" Celia demanded.

What? "No, hell, *no*."

"My life isn't some game. My emotions can't just be jerked around by you because you're in the mood to push my buttons." Her lips were red and plump from his kiss. Her eyes glittered with fury and passion.

"I wasn't—"

"In case you missed it before, Sullivan…" Her chin lifted. "Our marriage is *over*. You signed the divorce papers, remember?"

And he felt that shot, right in his heart. "Yes, I remember." He wished he could forget. *I thought I was doing the right thing. I was poison. She didn't need me.*

Though he'd always needed her.

"Get out of the elevator. When I need you, I'll be back."

He turned away from her. Exited that damn elevator. No one else was on the floor. It was way past operating hours. He wasn't even sure how she'd gotten up to his office.

Celia has her ways... Celia can do anything... Hadn't he heard folks say that about her time and again when he'd been working with the CIA?

Hell, most of his family didn't even know about the work he'd done for the government. Most of them didn't know a thing about Celia.

Mac knew.

And Sullivan...he'd tried so hard to forget her. An impossible task.

Before the elevator doors could shut, he lifted his hands, pushing against them. His gaze held hers. "What about when I need you?" It was a question torn from him.

She blinked in surprise. Or maybe in shock. A faint furrow appeared between her eyes.

"You said that...when you need *me*, you'd be back." Sullivan inclined his head toward her. "What about when I need you, C? What then?" Her old nickname rolled off his tongue. *C.* So simple, but...

It was our link. Only I called her that.

Back when she'd been his.

She laughed. It was a hollow, bitter sound. Not Celia's real laughter. He'd heard that light, musical sound once before. A lifetime ago. When would he hear her real laughter again?

"Oh, Sullivan," she said, her lips twisting in a cold smile. "We both know the truth. You've never really needed me. You wanted me for a time, but you never let me get close. When the chips were down, you turned on me."

Because he'd been told she betrayed him. Told again and again as his blood drained out in a dark, dank hell-hole.

"Don't do that again," she warned him. "Don't turn on me. I…I don't have a lot of options. I have to count on you."

"You can." He would *never* betray her again, and Sullivan would do whatever was necessary to prove that to her. He exhaled slowly and backed away. His hands fell back to his sides. The elevator doors began to close. "And just for the record…I think I need you more than I need anyone or anything else."

He saw the flash of surprise on her face.

Then the doors closed.

Breathe. Breathe. Breathe. Mentally, Celia James repeated her little mantra.

Only it was hard to breathe because she could still taste Sullivan. She could still feel his lips against hers. And when he'd dropped his last little bombshell on her, she was pretty sure her whole world had spun out of control.

She hurried across the darkened Austin street. She could hear the distant buzz of traffic. Random horns. Voices drifting on the wind. But…

Sullivan. Sexy Sullivan McGuire. *He* was what consumed her right then. And that was the problem with him—he always slipped past her guard. He always made her too nervous and aware. She couldn't afford the way he made her feel, not now. Not with all the other craziness happening in her life.

She was leaving the CIA. Leaving the agency that had been her life for far too long and…

I'm being hunted. She had enough going on without developing a new addiction to Sullivan.

Right…as if that were a *new* thing. She'd been craving him from the moment she looked into his green eyes. Then she'd heard the deep rumble of his voice. Seduction. Just straight-up seduction. She'd been lost before they'd even shaken hands and had been officially introduced.

She'd never looked up and just *wanted*. Until Sullivan, she'd always been so carefully controlled in all aspects of her life. But Sullivan had pretty much obliterated her control. He'd made her want to live for something other than the job.

When he'd left her, the job had been all she had left.

I won't make the same mistakes with him. Not this time. This time, she called the shots. He owed her.

Time had been kind to Sullivan. He was tall, fit, with powerful shoulders that had only gotten broader in the years they were apart. His dark hair was still thick, and her fingers had itched to slide through those heavy locks.

No, her fingers had just been itching to touch him. Sullivan had always attracted her. Like a moth to the flame, she'd been pulled right to him.

Not the same mistakes. Not!

Celia jumped into her car. She cranked the engine and drove away as fast as she could.

She'd only gone about four blocks before she realized she was being followed. That was four blocks too many. She should have spotted the tail instantly. But she'd been distracted…

By Sullivan.

Her hands tightened around the steering wheel.

She'd thought that she'd made a fairly clean escape when she'd sneaked down to Austin. She hadn't realized that the hunter on her trail had gotten so close.

And dammit, I led him straight to Sullivan.

Because if the guy on her trail had been waiting outside McGuire Securities…then he'd know about Sullivan and her connection to the McGuires. She'd gone to Sullivan for help. She hadn't intended to drag him straight into her nightmare. At least, not this fast.

She kept her left hand on the wheel even as her right activated the car's Bluetooth so she could call Sullivan. She'd memorized his cell number days ago—she had a knack for remembering pretty much everything. One of the reasons why she had been a good agent.

Had been.

He answered on the second ring. "Sullivan."

"It's me." She glanced in her rearview mirror. The headlights behind her were getting ever closer. Surely the guy wasn't going to hit her? Not on a public street.

"Celia, what—"

"Watch your back. I think I brought my trouble straight to your door. I—" The car behind rammed into her, and Celia's words ended in a sharp scream. Even as that cry escaped, she tightened her grip on the steering wheel and fought to keep her car steady.

"Celia? *Celia?*" Sullivan roared.

"Watch yourself," she said.

Her car had hurtled forward at the impact, but, thank goodness, she hadn't hit anyone or anything else. She shoved the gas pedal down as hard as she could. Her car shot forward, but the vehicle behind her, the one with the shining lights—

Killed the lights.

"Celia, what is happening?" Sullivan demanded.

She cut across the lanes, moving fast. She knew this city well, so she'd be able to disappear. Hopefully. But if that guy hit her again...

What is he thinking? Attacking in public?

"I've got company," she said as she fought to keep both her voice and the car steady. "The kind that isn't so friendly."

"Where are you?" he barked.

"Escaping," she told him honestly. And she was. She'd just turned down a dark side street. Celia turned off her own lights and whipped into the nearest parking garage. "Bye, Sullivan."

"No, Celia, wait—"

There was no time to wait. There was only time to survive. She was good at surviving. Celia jumped from her car and ran as fast as she could toward the shadows of the parking garage. She wouldn't have much time. She could already hear the engine of the other vehicle. An SUV waited a few feet away, and she rushed behind it, crouching down just as the squeal of tires reached her ears.

I knew my time was limited... I just didn't realize how close the hunter was to me.

Her heart slammed into her chest as the car braked just a few feet away. She reached into her boot and pulled out the knife she still kept strapped to her ankle.

Some habits sure did die hard.

She slipped around the SUV, keeping low and making certain not to make so much as a sound. The way she figured it, Celia had three options.

Option one...she could try to break into one of the parked cars and get a ride out of there. She would have to switch cars and temporarily *borrow* another if she went with the escape-in-a-vehicle option, because her car—with its busted bumper—wasn't going to get her far.

Option two…her eyes narrowed as she searched the garage's dim interior. Instead of stealing—um, borrowing—another car, she could rush for the nearest exit and escape on foot. Escaping on foot gave her a maneuverability advantage, but it sure wasn't the fastest option.

And, finally, she had option three.

She could fight.

Since she was armed with a knife and she had no idea what type of weapon the hunter had, fighting might not be—

"I know you're out there, Ms. James," a man's booming voice called. "So why don't you just save us both some time? Come out here…and let me put a bullet in your lovely head."

So he has a gun. Good to know.

"Because I have only one directive. Kill you. And I won't stop, not until you're dead."

That news was just rather unfortunate. Too bad for him, though. The unknown man wasn't going to achieve his directive any time soon—she had no intention of dying.

Her gaze slid to the red Exit sign she'd just spotted.

Knife versus gun wasn't such a good fighting option.

So I think I'll go with my second choice. Time to run…

"CELIA? CELIA?" SULLIVAN ROARED. But she wasn't answering him. The line had gone dead.

He shoved the phone back into his pocket, grabbed the white envelope she'd given him and then he rushed out of his office. He was in the elevator before he realized—hell, he had no idea where Celia was. He only knew she was in trouble. That she'd called him— telling him to watch his back.

And she'd screamed.

She could be hurt. And I don't know where she is. I can't help her.

The elevator took him to the ground floor. He rushed outside. Looked to the left. To the right. He didn't see anyone, but he wasn't going to stand there and keep making himself a target. He hurried to his car. Jumped inside.

"Celia..." Sullivan whispered her name as he cranked the vehicle and pulled away. "Where in the hell are you?"

Chapter Two

When he got home, Sullivan locked his door and reset his alarm. He'd driven around the damn city for far too long, searching in dark alleys, looking for any sign of Celia before he'd had to give up and head to his place.

He was sure that she'd been involved in some kind of accident. He'd heard what he *thought* was the crash and crunch of an impact when they'd been talking, but no accidents had been reported—he'd double-checked that with one of his contacts at the PD.

Celia had seemingly vanished.

Sighing, he turned on the lights. Tomorrow, he'd search for her again. He *would* find her.

"You're starting to go soft," Celia said, her voice calm and clear. "I mean, really, you didn't even know I was here?"

He spun around and found her sitting on his couch. She was leaning back against the cushions with her legs crossed in front of her, looking as if she didn't have a care in the world.

She's been here while I was searching the whole city for her? Frantic? He'd been imagining her broken body tossed away. And she'd been in his home.

"How long have you been here?" Sullivan asked

her. Her voice had been calm. His was tight with fury and fear.

Celia pursed her lips and glanced toward the clock near his TV. "About an hour. I was starting to think you must have been out with a hot date."

He stalked toward her. "I was out looking for *you*. I was tearing up the damn town because I thought you'd been hurt. I thought someone was after you and—"

"Someone was after me. Or rather, someone *is* after me." She didn't sound particularly worried. Her gaze held his. "A tail followed me from your office. He tried to take me. Or, actually, I think he was more interested in killing me than taking me. But that doesn't matter." She shrugged, moving her shoulders lightly against the leather of his couch. "He failed in his attempt."

Every muscle in his body locked down. "Take you?" Sullivan repeated. *"Kill you?"*

"Um...you know, the usual in our business. When forcing me off the road didn't work, he followed me into an old parking garage. I'd slipped inside there, thinking to use the place for shelter."

"Celia..."

"Like I said, he followed me. Jumped out of his vehicle. Gave me some nice line about how it would be easier if I just came out so he could put a bullet in my head."

His vision reddened as fury burned in his blood.

"I wasn't in the mood for that bullet, so I got away." Her words were said so simply. As if she hadn't just faced some life-or-death battle when he was far away and couldn't help her at all.

"How?" Sullivan demanded.

"The parking garage was dark, but it wasn't empty.

Other people approached from the elevator bank, so he had to put up his gun and act *not* killer-like. When I heard those folks approaching, I slipped away into the shadows and got out of there as fast as I could."

So the guy was still breathing. "He's a threat to you."

She just stared back at him.

"You saw him, though," Sullivan said, thinking quickly. "You got his description. With your contacts, you can find out who—"

"I didn't see him. I didn't stick around to get a full physical description. He had a gun, I had a knife, and with civilians in the area, I didn't want to risk them." Her fingers tapped along the arm of his couch. "So I left, without looking back. And as quickly as I could I…came here."

Her words gave him pause. "You came to me?" Sullivan stood about two feet away from her. He wanted to close that distance, scoop her up and hold her tight. Because he wanted that so badly, he kept his muscles locked and didn't move another step forward.

"I'm afraid I've brought you into this mess as a target. It's obvious that I went to McGuire Securities tonight, and if the guy after me has done any digging into my past, he'll know about you." She rose and came to stand right in front of him. "I'm sorry. I didn't mean to shine a bright target on you."

Sometimes, he forgot how delicate—physically— she was. She barely came to his shoulders as she stood there in her bare feet. He saw that she'd kicked her heels away, and they lay overturned next to his coffee table.

His hands lifted and his fingers curled around her shoulders. "You know I don't mind danger."

"That debt I was going to call in? It wasn't to protect me," she said. Had her eyes ever seemed bigger? Bluer? "I can protect myself. It was…I needed you to help me vanish."

He frowned at that bit of the news.

"I'm leaving the CIA. I've been compromised." She gave that bitter laugh again. The one that made him worry she'd changed—too much—since they were together. "Compromised again and again. I thought I could get away clean, but it sure seems my enemies aren't going to stop hunting me."

"You know who they are…"

"Actually, I don't. I've made a lot of enemies in my time at the agency. I joined right after college, was recruited straightaway. I was perfect for them, after all. No family. No close friends. No ties that would hold me back. I could become anyone they wanted me to be, and for a while, I did."

His hold tightened on her. "You have ties now."

"No, I don't. And that's why it was going to be so easy for me to leave."

But what had happened? Why was she quitting the agency? "The CIA was your life."

"Was it?" Her eyelashes flickered and then she seemed to notice that he was touching her. He felt her stiffen beneath his hands. "I'm sorry I broke into your place. After everything that went down tonight, I just needed to make sure you were all right."

She'd been worried…about him?

"But no one saw me enter your home. I was careful this time."

She pulled away. He let her go, but the temptation to hold her—it was far too strong.

"Maybe I will call in that debt you promised me

one day. My plans have changed now, so who knows?" She pushed back her hair, tucking a lock behind her left ear. "Remember what I said before, though. Watch your back."

She was walking away. Again. And he knew that if she slipped away, he wasn't going to see her again. Despite her words, she wouldn't be back to call in her debt. He suspected she wouldn't return to him at all. "Who is going to watch yours?" Sullivan wanted to know.

Celia tilted her head back as she gazed up at him. "Oh, Sully, be careful," she chided him. "It almost sounds as if you care about what happens to me."

I do. I never stopped caring, no matter how hard I tried. Some obsessions couldn't be conquered. "Stay here," he heard himself say, his voice way too gruff.

Celia shook her head. "What?"

He cleared his throat. "Stay the night. You said yourself that no one saw you come into my place. That means you're safe here. Stay the night. Get some sleep. Then you can make a new plan of attack or escape—or whatever the hell it is you want to do—in the morning."

She bit her lower lip. After a moment, voice strangely subdued, she said, "You know that's not a good idea."

"Do I?" It had sounded like one damn fine idea at the time.

"Yes." She sighed out that answer. "Sully, you know that—"

"I still want you." There. He'd said it. This time he wouldn't have lies or secrets between them. He'd tell her everything, because he wouldn't crash and burn again. Neither would she. Not on his watch.

"No." She put up her hand, as if to ward him off. "Stop it. Just…*stop it.*"

No way. He wasn't stopping. He could see her slipping away, and if she did—what would he do then? Go back to the bleak, empty world he'd been living in since he lost her before? Go back to looking at crowds—and always searching to see if he'd find her?

Mac had brought them back together on that last case. Sullivan had tried to warn his brother that he'd made a mistake. *How am I supposed to let her go again?* But Mac had been blind to the danger.

The simple truth was that Sullivan couldn't let Celia go. Not without losing too much of himself.

"I can't stop wanting you. Baby, I tried, but it just doesn't happen." He caught her hand in his and put it against his heart. A heart that always beat faster when she was near. "You think I don't know how much I screwed up before? I didn't trust you. I— Hell, I won't make the same mistake again. Give me a chance."

Her gaze searched his, but she shook her head. "I can't."

Those words—it felt as if she'd just driven her knife into his heart when she said them. The knife he knew she liked to keep strapped to her ankle.

"I can't go down this road with you again, Sully."

"I'm not talking about forever." He had asked for that, once. And he'd gotten it, with her. In a Vegas chapel, on one wild weekend. He'd promised forever to her.

I want it again.

But he knew he had to take small steps this time. "I'm talking one night. One night of safety for you. I have a guest room you can use. Just stay with me tonight. Tomorrow, we can make another plan together."

Maybe by tomorrow, he would have figured out a way to keep her with him.

"Hasn't your family been through enough?" Celia asked him. "Do you really want me and my danger close by?"

It wasn't about his family—and that alone told him just how far his obsession with her had gone. Family had always come first for him. The bond that he shared with his brothers and with his sister, Ava, was unbreakable, but…

But this isn't about them. It's about Celia.

"You have new evidence that can help you find your parents' killers," she said. "You should be sharing it with them and not—"

I haven't even opened the envelope. I was too worried about you. "It's almost midnight. Anything new I have can wait." Their parents had been waiting to receive justice for years. A few more hours wouldn't change anything. "Stay with me, Celia. I need to know you're safe tonight." And that was when he noticed the faint dark mark on her right cheek. His right hand lifted immediately and lightly touched that bruise. A bruise she *hadn't* possessed when she'd been in his office before.

"I think my cheek hit the steering wheel," she said, and Celia swallowed as his fingers lingered against her skin. "I got lucky—the air bag didn't deploy and I maintained control of my steering. If he'd hit me harder, the car could've died right there. He would've had me."

No one is getting you, Celia. I'm here now. "You saved my life once," he reminded her.

She gave a quick, hard shake of her head. "No, that's—"

"Did you think Mac didn't tell me? He did." *And as a thank-you, I signed divorce papers.* Dammit, could he have been more of a blind fool? He had so much to atone for with Celia. If he could just convince her to give him a chance...

"Your brother talks too much," she muttered darkly.

He laughed at those words. Sullivan just couldn't help it. Mac was pretty much the definition of the strong, silent type. The only guy more closemouthed than Mac?

That would be me.

Her face softened a bit as she stared up at him. "You should do that more, you know."

"What?"

"Laugh. Let go of that iron control of yours and just enjoy life."

His laughter faded away. "Maybe you should follow the same advice." *And you should stay with me. Just for the night.* "Are you always on guard?" Sullivan asked her.

Her dimples flashed, but her smile wasn't real. "You tell me. You lived in my world for a few months. Is it really the kind of place where you can let down your guard?"

He'd joined the CIA and worked in the Special Activities Division, or SAD, as the group was called. He'd been undercover, working to make a difference, desperately trying to collect needed intelligence in a hostile country—only that case had gone to hell, fast. Friends had become enemies, and he'd found himself on the run.

Then...captured.

Tortured.

Left for dead.

"You can let your guard down with me, Celia. Trust me, just for this night," he told her. Because now he could see the edge of fear that she'd been working so hard to conceal at his office. And…she was pale. Shadows were under her eyes, shadows that even the careful application of makeup couldn't hide.

She needed rest. She needed safety.

I want her to need me.

"Just for the night," Celia said. "Only that."

He actually shook his head because he hadn't thought she'd agree, but— "You'll stay with me?"

"Just for the night," she said again. "Come morning, I have plans."

She pulled away from him and headed toward his hallway. "Which one is the guest room?"

It took a moment for her question to register. She'd never been in his house before, so she didn't know her way around. They'd been married, but…he hadn't brought her to his home. He hadn't introduced her to his family. He'd said his *I do* part to her, then taken a mission almost the next day. He'd been shipped out of the country. She'd been scheduled to follow him two days later.

But…everything had changed.

"The third door," he said. "On the left."

She looked back. "That better not turn out to be your bedroom there, Marine. Because trusting you to give me a place to crash tonight is *not* the same thing as trusting you in bed."

If only.

"My bedroom is the first door." Had his voice been too gruff? Maybe. The thought of her in his bed had made him sound too rough.

She turned away.

He called out, "But feel free to go in there. Because you can trust me on this…if you go to my room, I will give us both what we need."

If she'd give him the chance, he'd give her everything. Anything she wanted.

"Don't hold your breath on that one," Celia threw back at him. Then she vanished down the hallway.

His breath expelled on a long rush. *I've got you in my house, baby. That's step one…*

"YOU LOST CELIA JAMES?"

Porter Vance winced as he heard the rage, transmitted so very clearly over the phone. "Look, boss, the woman is CIA. It's not like she isn't trained to—"

"*You're* ex-CIA. You're supposed to understand her moves. You're supposed to find her and eliminate her. End of story."

Porter glanced around the busy intersection. The parking garage was behind him—the garage that contained Celia's abandoned vehicle. "You were right, you know," he said, trying to distract the boss. "She did go to see Sullivan McGuire. That's where I found her. I just parked myself right outside McGuire Securities and she damn near came running out of the business and straight at me. I trailed her, had her in the parking garage on Forty-Seventh Street and then…" He cleared his throat.

"Then you lost her. A woman that I paid you ten thousand dollars to eliminate."

Right. He hadn't exactly gotten the money yet. It was one of those pay-on-delivery deals. So far, he hadn't delivered a dead Celia James. "I'll get her. Listen, I'm already back at McGuire Securities. She'll show here again. If she doesn't, I'll just use Sullivan to get her. She's still tied to him. He can be the bait. When she knows I've got him, she'll come running to me."

Laughter carried across the line. "Sullivan isn't easy prey. None of the McGuires are…but especially not *him*."

There was something in the boss's voice…

"Do you think I didn't try to eliminate him? Do you honestly think I didn't do my best to kill that guy when I had the chance?"

"I—"

"Your usefulness is at an end."

It took a moment for those cold words to sink in.

And another minute to realize…

I've been shot.

Because the bullet had been so quiet as it found its mark. There was no bang. No boom. Just a faint whistle as it cut through the air and sank into Porter's chest.

And then the pain came, burning slowly through his heart.

He looked down. It was dark there, too dark for him to see clearly but—

My shirt is wet. I'm bleeding.

He still had the phone in his hand. Still had it pressed to his ear. But his legs were crumpling and Porter knew…the boss had called him so that he'd be distracted. The boss had already known he'd failed at his mission.

And the boss didn't accept failure.

He was watching me. He called… He was going to kill me, no matter what I told him. Maybe because he'd just been another loose end.

Just like Celia.

The phone fell from his fingers and he crashed onto the concrete.

Chapter Three

"Will you marry me, Celia?"

She lay in bed, the covers pulled up to her chin, and the past wouldn't stop haunting her.

"Don't tease, Sully. When you say that to a woman, she might just take you up on the offer." They'd been in Vegas. Bright lights. Slot machines. Parties that didn't stop.

The champagne hadn't stopped, either.

But she hadn't been drunk. She couldn't pretend that she had. Sully...

"I'm not teasing." His handsome face had been dead serious. That wonderful square jaw of his had been hard with determination. His green gaze had seemed to see straight into her soul. *"I want to be with you, C. Tonight and always. Marry me?"*

Her hold tightened on the covers. There were no rings on her fingers—not any rings at all. But he'd given her one that night. When they'd pulled up at that little chapel. When she'd been almost delirious with happiness. When she hadn't been able to stop smiling.

"I love you." Her words, to him. She should have known, even then, that it wouldn't work. Because Sullivan hadn't told her that he loved her. He'd held that

part back. He'd kissed her wildly. Made love to her endlessly that night. But…

But did he ever love me?

She wasn't sure that he had.

And now she was in his home. In his spare bedroom. And she couldn't stop thinking about *him*.

"This isn't working." The sound of her own voice was jarring, but maybe she needed to be jarred. Because for her to just agree to stay with him—how wrong was that? She knew exactly how bad the guy was for her. She'd gone to his office because—yes, she actually had planned to use him. He had connections in Mexico, and she'd intended to call in her favor when she slipped over the border. She hadn't planned to wind up in Sullivan's bed.

Celia dressed as quickly as she could. As soon as she was gone, her first order of business would be finding new clothes. Maybe changing her hair again. Red was actually her natural color, but by the time she cleared the border, she intended to be a brunette. Maybe a brunette with green eyes? It'd be easy to pick up some contacts and then she'd nearly be a new person.

Again.

She tiptoed into the hallway. Celia figured she'd been in the guest room for nearly an hour, maybe two, tossing and turning and replaying her past too many times. Sullivan would be asleep by now, and she'd sneak out of his house as quickly and easily as she'd slipped in. But maybe she'd leave the guy a note, telling him that he really needed to install a few new security measures. The setup was good, but *not* good enough and—

"Celia."

She froze in front of his open bedroom door. He'd

spotted her. It wasn't pitch-black in the hallway. Light spilled in from the den, illuminating the narrow corridor. She turned her head and stepped toward his room, her movements still soundless. She started to speak.

"Celia, don't go."

Words froze in her throat.

He sounded so desperate. When had Sullivan ever been desperate? She inched closer, her chest seeming to burn, and then—

Moonlight spilled through his blinds, revealing his form in that big, sprawling bed. Sullivan's muscular chest was bare, and the sheets were tangled around his hips. He was rolling a bit in the bed, and his eyes were *closed.*

Surprise held her motionless.

Sullivan had picked up a few habits since they'd last been together. It seemed that he now talked in his sleep. And he dreamed about…her.

A low warmth bloomed in her belly.

She found herself stepping toward him. The floor creaked beneath her feet. Celia froze, but it was too late.

So much for being quiet.

Sullivan instantly shot up in bed.

"Sully—"

In an instant he had his hands on her. She could have escaped his hold. Could have fought and had *him* tumbling back, but she didn't. He caught her in his arms and pinned her between his body and the door frame.

"Celia?" His hands slid over her. "What is it? What's happening?"

Oh, just the usual. I was sneaking away in the middle of the night. She wet her lips and tried to figure out a nice excuse that might work. And one that just might not make her seem like the coward she was.

He wasn't holding her prisoner any longer, not now that recognition and consciousness had hit him fully. In fact, he'd backed up a bit so that his body wasn't touching hers at all. But he was still there, a strong, immovable object in her path, and the heat from his body seemed to wrap around her. Her hand lifted and her fingers slid over his chest.

She hadn't meant to touch him…had she?

He called for me in his sleep.

Her fingers trailed over his chest, and she felt the raised marks on his skin. "You didn't have these scars before." She knew she was touching scars. In her business, you could always recognize them. Carefully now, she slid her hand down and felt more scars along his ribs. Another near his stomach. Another—

His hand locked around her wrist. "Be careful just how far you go." In the darkened room, his eyes glittered at her.

She swallowed the lump in her throat. "Did you get those scars when you were captured?" The last mission he'd worked with the CIA. The mission that had changed *everything*.

Traitors had been revealed. Loyalties had been tested. And when the blood and dust finally cleared, he'd left her.

And she'd picked up the pieces and carried on.

"My captors wanted information." His voice was a hard growl, but his fingers were lightly stroking the inside of her wrist. Could he feel her skyrocketing pulse? "They were real interested in learning everything they could about the Special Activities Division."

"I didn't betray you." Hadn't she told him that before? When she'd finally gotten him on the phone after that brutal mission. He'd refused to see her when she tried to visit him at the hospital. Mac had gruffly turned her away, but she'd finally gotten Sullivan on the phone and—

It's over, Celia.

Her eyes closed. Her cheeks burned. "Why couldn't you have trusted me?"

"Because I'd spent seven days in a hellhole. They'd sliced me open. They'd nearly killed me—again and again—and all the while, they kept telling me things that only *you* should know. They told me you'd been playing me, from the very beginning. That you'd sent me out there, knowing they'd capture me. That you weren't on that transport with me because you were keeping your cover in place. That everything that happened to me...it was because of you."

Pain hit her so much harder than she'd anticipated. So hard it stole her breath and left her gasping. "I didn't... I wouldn't! I'd never—*not to you!*" How could he have thought, even for a moment, that she'd done that to him? That she'd married him one day then betrayed him the next?

"I was in hell, C. *Hell.* Barely alive when Mac pulled me out."

"I know," she rasped. "I was there. Who do you think drove the getaway jeep?" But he should know that. Mac had said—

"What?" Stunned surprise was in his voice.

"I was there. Don't act like Mac didn't tell you. I know he did." She'd been there, and she'd seen the blood on him, but she hadn't been given the chance to fully take stock of all his injuries. She'd been too busy driving hell fast to get them to safety. Then the transport chopper had whisked him away and she'd stood below, watching the dust and sand billow around him. There hadn't been enough room for her and Mac on that chopper. So she'd backed away and let Mac stay with his brother.

And when she'd finally gotten back to him…

It's over, Celia. She tried to slam the door on that memory before it hurt her even more.

"Mac told me…he said that you used intel to find me…that you helped…but hell, no, he never said you were there." Sullivan sounded stunned.

"I was there." And she'd heard his words so clearly as she'd driven that jeep. *It was…Celia. Never trust… her.* "I didn't give up on you. I wouldn't have." Even if he'd given up on her. She fought to keep her emotions under control. She had to get away from him. Staying had been a definite mistake. But she couldn't stop herself from saying, "You were a marine, first and foremost. You should have known that you can't trust your captors. They always try to make you turn on the people you *should* be trusting." It was a basic rule of survival. Never trust them.

"They knew so many things about you," Sullivan said. "About us. Things I'd only told *you*."

They were lying. "I need to leave." This wasn't working. In fact, she felt as if she were about to splinter apart. "Get out of my way and let me go."

He didn't move. "You were running from me, weren't you? Trying to slip away in the dark? You were going to vanish without saying good-bye."

Her chin notched up. Could he see that little movement? "No, I wasn't just going to vanish," she said flatly. "I was strongly thinking about leaving you a note first."

And then he was touching her. Sullivan put his hands on her shoulders and pushed her back against that door frame once more. His heat scorched her. "A note?" His voice was strangled. *"A note?"*

"Let me go." Or he'd find out just how strong she was.

"I can't. I tried that before, but you came back, and now we're both in trouble." Then his head lowered toward hers. She expected a kiss. Hard. Angry. Passionate. She wasn't going to respond to him. She wasn't.

But his mouth didn't crash down onto hers.

Instead, his lips…feathered over her neck. Over the pulse that raced so frantically, for him. He kissed her skin lightly, tenderly, moving in a sensual trail along the column of her neck.

He remembered.

Even after all the time that had passed, he still remembered how much she'd enjoyed it when he kissed her there. How the passion had spiraled inside her from such a tender touch.

A moan built in her throat and slipped free before she could hold it back.

"I love that sound," he whispered against her. "I missed it."

Her eyes had squeezed shut. She wondered how the world had gotten so out of control. Once, she'd nearly had everything she wanted. Now…everything had been ripped away. Tears stung her lashes, but she'd never let those tears fall.

She couldn't.

"Celia, I want you."

Wanting had never been their problem.

I want him so much right now that I'm shaking.

But taking him wasn't an option. Was it?

His hands slid down her arms, moving closer to her elbows, and she felt the edge of his fingertips skim over the curve of her breasts. She sucked in a sharp breath. "Sully…"

"Do you know how many times you've been in my dreams?"

Her eyes opened. She blinked the moisture away. "You were dreaming about me tonight. I heard you." His call had stopped her.

"And that's why you didn't run away? Why you came to me?"

No, she hadn't been going to him. She'd just wanted to make sure he was all right. "I thought you were calling out to me."

"I've called out to you a hundred times, but this is the first time you've heard me."

His words didn't make sense to her. "Sully…"

"I love it when you say my name like that."

"I can't." *Can't be with you. Can't do this.* "Goodbye." Then, yes, she jerked from his arms and pretty much ran from that room. She—

His phone was ringing. A loud, hard music beat that followed her.

She paused, escape so close but…*no calls this late are ever a good sign.* She looked back in time to see a light flash on—Sullivan had turned on his lamp.

Sullivan grabbed his phone from the nightstand,

yanking it off the charger. "Sullivan." The light from the lamp spilled around him.

Naked. The man is totally naked.

She'd just had that long talk with a naked man. No wonder he'd grabbed her wrist when she'd been searching for his scars. She'd almost touched something a whole lot bigger than a scar.

"What? In front of our building? Hell, no, that can't be… Listen, more is going on here. It's…" His gaze cut toward her. "Celia is with me," he said. "She was chased tonight. She thinks some bozo followed her from our office. Yeah, yeah…" His hold tightened on the phone. "My gut says there is a connection, too. I'll be right down there. I want to see the guy."

She inched closer to him. As soon as he lowered the phone, Celia demanded, "What happened?"

"That was Mac. A man was killed right in front of McGuire Securities, shot in the heart. Mac is down there now because a cop buddy tipped him off."

Her breath came a little faster. "You don't buy that the guy's death is a coincidence, do you?"

"After what went down with you tonight? Hell, no, I don't. I want you to see the body. *I* want to see him."

She shook her head. "I told you already, I didn't get a look at the guy after me tonight."

"No, but that doesn't mean you don't know him. It wouldn't be the first time someone in the agency decided to turn traitor."

"I heard his voice." And she hadn't recognized it.

"And I've heard you adopt nearly a dozen accents at will. Voices can be disguised. I want to see this guy. Once we get an up-close look at him, we'll know more."

She cleared her throat. "And I'd, um, really appreciate it if you'd cover up."

He glanced down at himself and swore. Then he grabbed a sheet and wrapped it around his hips. "Happy now?"

"Not really." She edged a bit closer to him. "But I'm going with you. Have they already transferred the body?"

"Mac says they're working on that now. But don't worry, I've got a friend who will give us access at the medical examiner's office."

She knew exactly how well connected the McGuire family was in Austin. "If it is the guy who was after me," Celia said, her mind spinning, "then how'd he wind up dead?"

Sullivan just stared back at her, and she could almost hear his suspicions.

"It wasn't me," she snapped. "I didn't kill him."

"Celia—"

"But why would you believe me, right?" She turned away. "Forget it. *I'll* call Mac. He can take me to the body. You just stay here."

"You don't need my brother's help. You have me."

She glanced back at him. *No, I don't.*

"And I never said I thought you'd killed anyone. But you haven't told me why the man was gunning for you."

I don't know why. I just know that he's been coming after me. My home wasn't safe, so I had to run, fast. And I ran to you.

A move that had been a serious mistake.

"I'm trying to figure all this out," Sullivan said. "Maybe the dead man was just the flunky doing the dirty work and someone else is out there pulling the strings."

Her lips pressed together. She had the same suspicion that he did. Maybe the guy's boss had gotten fed up with his failure.

"Perhaps his employer didn't like to hear that you'd slipped away." Sullivan was dressing now, yanking on jeans and a T-shirt. "Maybe that made him so angry that he decided to take out that frustration on someone."

And he'd killed a man? Unfortunately, she knew just how often events like this occurred. That knowledge was one of the reasons she was ready to escape the dark world she'd lived in for so long.

A woman could only handle so much death and despair before they started to choke the life from her.

HE'D CALLED THE authorities and anonymously left a tip about the body's location. If he hadn't, it would have been dawn before Porter's body was discovered. He hadn't wanted to waste that much time.

Celia James was off the grid. He needed to get her back in the game ASAP. And a dead body pretty much dropped at her ex-lover's business? That should snag her attention.

Especially since I think Sullivan is helping Celia once more.

But it wasn't Sullivan McGuire who raced to the scene when the blue lights first appeared on Austin Street. It was Sullivan's older brother, Mac. A foe just as dangerous.

From the shadows, he watched as Mac talked with the cops, acting as if he was old friends with them. Probably because he was. The McGuires had gotten in deep with the cops while trying to unmask their parents' killers.

And you still haven't found them, have you?

He smiled at that thought. *What would you do, Mac, if you knew I was right there when your parents were shot? I'm across the street from you right now. So close, and you haven't got a clue...*

And Sullivan...blind Sullivan...he'd been in the same room with the guy before. He'd worked missions with Sullivan, and the guy had been completely in the dark.

Porter's body was being loaded up now. He'd been zipped up and was being placed in a van for transport to the coroner's office. Mac headed back to his car, seemingly leaving the scene.

This can't be it.

The guy wasn't just going to walk away. But...wait, Mac *had* called someone before. He'd seen him place the call. Had Mac phoned Sullivan?

And when the medical examiner's van pulled away from the scene, he saw Mac leave in his vehicle and tail that van.

Ah...*going after the body.* That made sense. Mac would try to ID the fellow. And as the watcher shifted position, he realized, *I bet Sullivan will go after the body, too.*

His plan was working. He just needed to trail behind, carefully, and see what happened next. Celia would show herself soon enough, and then she'd be the one loaded into the back of the medical examiner's van.

THE MEDICAL EXAMINER'S office was cold. Icy. From the corner of his eye, Sullivan saw Celia shiver. He wanted to wrap his arms around her, but he doubted she'd appreciate that gesture, so…he shrugged out of his coat and put it around her shoulders.

She glanced over at him, her eyebrows shooting up.

"You were cold," he said simply.

Her fingers caught the coat. "Thank you."

He offered her a smile. "I brought you to a morgue, C. It's not like I took you out on some fancy date. I should—"

"We've never gone on a fancy date."

Her words gave him pause. Then he realized…hell, she was right. They'd worked missions. They'd ridden out hard and desperate adrenaline highs together. They'd shared passionate nights that were permanently singed in his memory.

But I never took the woman out on a real date?

He would never dig himself out of the hole he'd dug. "I'm sorry," Sullivan said gruffly. "If I could go back in time, there are about a million things I'd do differently with you."

Her gaze cut away from him.

"Celia…about our marriage…" It was definitely past time he cleared up a few issues there. "You need to know why I proposed."

She laughed. The bitter laugh. The *not* Celia laugh. "You were drunk. We'd both worked too many cases. We were both—"

"You said you loved me."

"No." Her voice was hard. Cold.

And something inside him died. *She didn't love me? She—*

"We are not doing this here. We are not talking about our past, about my feelings for you, in a morgue! It's dark, you snuck me in here like we were robbers, and the place smells. This isn't where we have that conversation, got it?"

He cleared his throat. "I, um, got it." But his lips were quirking. How had he forgotten her wonderful bite? Damn, but he could fall for her again so easily.

The doors to the morgue swung open. A gurney was pushed inside by a whistling man who seemed totally oblivious of their presence.

Sullivan had a quick déjà vu moment. He'd flipped on his own lights and found Celia just waiting for him.

But then the man pushing the gurney glanced over at them and offered a broad smile, and Sullivan realized this wasn't some county employee.

"What in the hell?" Sullivan demanded. "Mac?"

His brother shrugged. "Figured you'd be waiting inside. I told the ME to take a little break." He pushed the gurney forward and paused to pull on a pair of gloves. "We are so screwing with the chain of evidence here, so don't touch him, okay? Just look at the body, nothing more."

The chain of evidence? Yeah, they were messing with it, all right. Because they weren't supposed to be there, but…when Mac lowered the zipper and Celia gave a sharp, indrawn breath, Sullivan knew that his instincts had been dead-on.

"You recognize him," Sullivan said.

"Hi, Celia," Mac murmured. "Good to see you again…"

She inched closer to the body, but she made no move to touch the dead man. "His hair should be blond, not black. But yes, yes, I know him." She looked up at Sullivan. "I trained him, right after you left. He was my next assignment."

Because Celia was a handler. She brought in the new agents. Trained them. Guided them.

"Porter Vance," she said softly. "He can't be the man who tried to kill me. He had no reason to come after me!"

"He appears to have been staking out McGuire Securities…" Mac said.

"Just like the guy who followed me earlier," Celia murmured.

"And he had a gun," Mac added. "It was found on scene, so I think it's safe to say the fellow wasn't just hanging around for some friendly little chat." Mac's voice was curt. His green eyes were solemn as he stared back at her, and his face was tense.

Celia glanced over at Sullivan. "You think he was there to kill me. That he was waiting for me to show again?" Her gaze slid back to Mac. "That's what you both think?"

"I don't think he was there selling Girl Scout cookies," Mac drawled.

Sullivan forced his back teeth to unclench. "He was lying in wait, Celia." It was the only thing that made sense to him. "You gave him the slip before, so he went back to McGuire Securities. Maybe he thought I'd lead him to you."

"But someone took Porter out instead," Mac said. "So either someone was protecting you, Celia, or someone shut this guy up so he couldn't reveal anything about who wanted you dead." He paused just a moment. "I realize it's been a while since Sully and I have been in the business, so I don't know…just how many enemies have you made lately?"

She'd paled as she stared at the dead man. Sullivan

studied the guy. Porter Vance appeared to be in his thirties, maybe late twenties. He had short hair, a muscular build and a bullet hole in his chest.

"I didn't think Porter was my enemy," Celia said softly. "He had no reason to want me dead. He was… he was one of the good guys." Her right hand lifted and she rubbed her temple. "At least, I thought he was."

Mac glanced over at Sullivan. "One shot, straight through the heart. I talked with the forensics team on scene. Based on the angle of entry and the bullet used, they think it was a sniper shot, probably from the building directly across the street. Porter probably never saw the attack coming." He inclined his head. "A smashed burner phone was found beneath the body. No ID was on the fellow, but like I said before, he was armed. The cops took his gun into evidence." Then he glanced at his watch. "Our five minutes are nearly up. We need to clear out of here, now." He zipped the bag back up.

"Porter," Celia said his name again. "This just doesn't make sense to me. He left the CIA a year ago. There's no reason for him to come after me!"

But he was there.

And he'd tried to kill her that night.

"Porter was always good with voices and accents," Celia muttered as she kept rubbing her temple. "Even better than me. I should have remembered that. He was one of the chameleons. He could become anyone on command." Her lashes lowered. "Just like me."

"Okay…again…" Mac cleared his throat and glanced over his shoulder. "Our five minutes are about up. I promised we'd be out of here. Our presence can't exactly be widely known, unless you want to explain to all the authorities just who Celia is."

No, he didn't intend to explain her to anyone. They'd sneaked in the back door and his contact had let him in. Only one person had seen Celia so far. Others would be arriving soon, so it was definitely time to go.

"We have a starting point now," Sullivan told Celia as he caught her elbow and steered her toward the door. "We start with him and we work back. We can figure this out." They were in the hallway now, and Mac was following close behind them.

"There's no *we* in this thing," Celia said. She squared her shoulders. "Your part is done. I obviously made a mistake contacting you. Don't you see that? There was a dead body dropped—almost literally—on your doorstep." She shook her head. "I should have just emailed you the information about your parents and not tried to work a deal."

"Uh, our parents?" Mac demanded. "Just what information do you have on them, Celia?"

Her gaze cut to him. "I know why your mother entered the Witness Protection Program. I know who she was before she changed names and moved across the country. I know the real reason she was running."

Mac took an aggressive step forward. "And that reason would be?"

Celia looked back at Sullivan.

I haven't opened the envelope yet. He'd waited because he wanted to share that information when his family was all together. And because he'd been too tangled up in her. "I was calling a family meeting in the morning," he explained quietly. "Things got a little…out of control, so I didn't get to call you."

"Right, *out of control*." Mac nodded. "I can see that. Dead bodies can lead to a loss of control."

Celia was hurrying down the hallway.

"So can sexy ghosts from your past," Mac added.

After shooting a glare at his brother, Sullivan took off after her. He'd only taken a few steps when Mac grabbed his arm. "Maybe you need to let her go."

"Are you kidding me?" Sullivan gaped at him. "You're the one who told me I made a mistake! You're—"

"I'm the one who saw how much you hurt her before. And I'm the one who doesn't want to see her in pain again. If you aren't serious about her, you need to just back off. She's got enough to deal with now as it is."

An enemy—one killing in the shadows. "She won't even tell me why she's being targeted. It's like she doesn't trust me."

Mac laughed. "Well, I guess that means you know how she felt before, right? Sucks, doesn't it? When someone turns on you?"

He heard the clatter of her heels. She was at the end of the hallway. A few more moments, and Celia would be outside.

But we came in my car. It's not like she'll hot-wire it and leave me.

Hell. She would.

He shoved his brother aside and rushed after her.

She opened the door. Darkness waited.

"Celia!" Sullivan yelled. "Don't—"

There was a whistle of sound, then a *thunk*. Wood flew into the air—splintering away from the door—even as Celia dove back inside the building. She hit the floor before he could reach her. Sullivan was pretty sure that his heart stopped when she slammed into the ground.

The bullet didn't hit her. The bullet didn't hit her.

He grabbed her arms and yanked her away from the still-open door. He held her close, his grip probably too tight, but he didn't care, and he backed down the hall-way as fast as he could.

"What in the hell was that?" Mac snarled.

"That…" Celia huffed out a hard breath. Her body was tense against Sullivan's. "That was someone who wants me dead. And that bullet would have hit me if Sully hadn't called my name."

And in that last instant, she'd turned back. She'd moved back toward him. The bullet had missed her head and hit the door.

Too close. Too close.

"This is a county facility!" Mac's grating voice seemed to echo around them. "To attack here…this guy is freaking insane."

Insane…or just very, very determined to take out his target.

And now Sullivan realized just why Porter had been killed and left at McGuire Securities. "The shooter knew we'd come to look at the body. He wanted to draw you out so he could—"

"Try to kill me?" Celia finished. She glanced up at Sullivan, her dark lashes making her blue eyes appear even brighter. "Yes, I figured that out, too. Right after the bullet nearly lodged in my head."

It was hard to breathe. *She can't die.* "You're not running from me," Sullivan rasped.

Mac was on his phone. Probably getting all his cop buddies ready to search the scene out there. The shooter had missed, though, and Sullivan was betting he wasn't just going to sit around while the authorities closed in. No, he'd flee, for the moment.

And then come back for another attack.

"You're not running," Sullivan said again. "You're going to tell me exactly what's going on. Why you're on some nut job's hit list… And then *we* are going to stop him." He'd let her down once before. He'd be damned if he did it again.

Chapter Four

The McGuire ranch.

Celia shivered a bit as Sullivan's car headed down the winding drive that led to the main ranch. She'd never been out to the ranch. Never met any of Sullivan's family—well, except for Mac. Mac knew plenty of her secrets.

But after the shooting, Sullivan had insisted she head out to the ranch. And after her discovery about Porter's identity and that near bullet to the head, she'd needed a safe haven.

Havens didn't get much safer than the McGuire ranch.

She knew all about the dark history of that ranch. Years ago, Sullivan and his brothers had all left home— they'd gone out, trying to save the world, in their own ways.

Grant McGuire, the eldest brother, had been a lethal Army Ranger. Davis and Brodie—the twins—had both excelled as Navy SEALs. Mac...he'd been Delta Force, as cold and deadly as a man could be. Then Sullivan, the youngest of the brothers, had signed up to be a marine.

She'd tapped into their files during her time at the CIA. She'd read accounts of their dangerous missions.

She'd been impressed—and a little awed—by all that they'd accomplished.

At the CIA, she'd actually been the one to suggest recruiting both Mac and Sullivan. Their exploits had caught her attention. She'd been the one to bring Sullivan into the nightmare… *It was my fault he was taken.*

Her fingers twisted in her lap. Yes, she'd been the one to do all the digging into Sullivan's life. She'd been the one to first put him on the CIA's radar.

It started with me.

They drew closer to the ranch. The sun had risen and she easily saw all the vehicles parked there. The whole family had obviously gathered for this meeting.

They're not here for me. I'm just the tagalong. They're all gathered to learn about the past.

Sullivan was going to share the information she'd given to him about his mother. The McGuires would continue their search for justice.

While I hide.

Oh, how the mighty had fallen.

She exhaled slowly and peered up at the house. It had been rebuilt, rather extensively, by Brodie and Davis. She really knew far too much about the McGuire family. But learning about them…it had been almost a compulsion for her.

Because of Sullivan.

While Sullivan and his brothers were out protecting the world, evil had come to the ranch. Sullivan's mother and father had been gunned down in their own home, and Ava—the baby of the family—had been forced to bear the brunt of the tragedy. For years, rumors had swirled that Ava had even been involved in their deaths.

She hadn't been.

She'd been a victim.

There are so many victims.

Sullivan braked the vehicle near the main house. He killed the engine and turned his attention toward her.

"Thanks for giving me a place to stay," Celia said softly. "I won't be here long. I just need to pull some intel together and then I'll be—"

"I've already told you." His voice was a rough growl that made goose bumps rise on her skin. The rather good kind of goose bumps. "You're not running from me again."

I didn't run before.

Her gaze slid from his and headed toward the house once more. A man had just come out. Like Sullivan, he was tall, with dark hair and broad shoulders. "What are you going to tell them about me?"

"What do you want me to tell them?"

Her index finger tapped against the side of the door. "Do they know you were married to me?"

"No."

That hurt. But she wouldn't let him know that he'd just ripped into her heart. She forced a smile to her lips and turned toward him. "Of course they don't. It was really just a brief thing. A mistake easily forgotten."

His eyes narrowed.

"I don't think they need to know anything about our past." Maybe her words came too quickly, but she was suddenly desperate to get out of that car and put some distance between them. "Just tell them I'm a client. I can even pay you, if you want. Make it legit so you don't have to lie to your family."

"Celia…"

She shoved open her door and bolted from the vehicle. Mac had followed a bit behind them, and she heard the approach of his car. She was pretty grateful for his timely arrival. Mac had always been a friend to her.

She could really use a friend right now.

Sullivan slammed his door and hurried to her side. She stiffened her spine and glanced up at him with raised eyebrows. All in all, it had been one heck of a night, and the morning wasn't looking much better for her.

He never told them about the marriage. In case there had been any doubt, now she knew with certainty—he really hadn't cared about her.

"While you talk to your family, I just need a quiet place to make a phone call." She'd picked up a burner phone before they'd left the city. The cops—and Mac—had searched for the shooter, but he'd been long gone. She'd had to watch from the shadows while that search was conducted. She hadn't wanted to talk with the cops. That would just have been a complication she didn't need.

That shooting had been too close for comfort. *Another step forward, and I would have been gone.*

So maybe her night hadn't been as bad as it *could* have been.

"I want you with me."

The dark-haired man on the porch had been joined by another guy—a guy who looked exactly like him.

The twins. And they were both staring at her a bit suspiciously. Wonderful. If they knew that she had a man gunning for her—literally—she was sure they'd look even less welcoming.

Hello, there. My name's Celia. And I just brought death to your door. Oh, yes, they'd love her.

She just knew how to make a killer first impression.

Sullivan's hand reached for hers. Instinctively, she stepped back.

Pain flashed on his face.

Join the club, buddy.

"Celia?" Sullivan whispered. "What's wrong?"

She started to bite her lip but then thought—*why?* There was no need to hold back any longer. She had nothing to lose. "Oh, let me see... I just found out that the man I married decided I was so beneath him that he never bothered to tell his family about our wedding. I mean I get it," she snapped, anger pulsing through her. "You thought I was part of the group that set you up. I wasn't. I went in to save your ungrateful butt, but you wouldn't listen to me."

A car braked behind her. She looked back and saw Mac.

She didn't calm down. "Mac knew the truth. He never thought I was some terrible double agent out to kill you." Her heart was about to burst out of her chest. "Why could he trust me?"

Mac was climbing from his car now and closing in.

"Why could he," she pushed, "but not you?"

"Because I was a fool."

That answer just wasn't good enough. She looked back toward the porch. At his brothers. The family she was supposed to just meet with a fake smile. "I can't do this." Not anymore. Wasn't that why she was getting out of the game? Leaving the CIA? Because she was just *done*. "I'm going to the guesthouse." She spun on her heel.

"You...know where it is?"

She laughed and glanced over her shoulder. "Hi,

there," she said with a little wave at Sullivan. "I'm CIA, remember?" Well, *ex*-CIA. "It wasn't exactly hard to research your family and home. So, yes, I know about the guesthouse. And I'm heading there." Not into the fire of his home with his family. "When you're done… hell, don't come to me, okay?" She turned and focused on Mac. "After your family talk, will *you* come and get me?" Mac owed her. She'd helped him *and* his bride-to-be, Elizabeth. And that case—well, it had been the final straw for her.

"What's going on?" Mac wanted to know.

She could only shake her head. She'd just been pushed too far. Too hard. Her life was hanging in the balance, and Sullivan—

Will the pain ever stop?

Sullivan reached out and locked his fingers around her arm. She froze. Her frantic gaze met Mac's.

His jaw hardened. "Let her go, Sully," Mac ordered.

"You want to stay out of this," Sullivan warned him. "This is between me and Celia."

"No, it isn't. Because she's my friend. She has been, for a long time."

She kept her expression schooled to show no emotion.

"Let her go," Mac said again. Then, voice lower, "Sully, can't you see that you're hurting her?"

And instantly, Sullivan let her go. She marched forward, moving almost woodenly. She'd gotten maps of the property before. She knew where the guesthouse was located. But, despite her words to Sullivan, she didn't head there. Instead, she walked toward the bluff that overlooked the nearby lake.

One step. Then another.

She didn't look back at Sullivan.

SULLIVAN COULDN'T TAKE his eyes off Celia. "I didn't mean to hurt her."

But he had. Her eyes had swum with tears. He didn't think that he'd ever seen Celia cry, but she'd just come very, very close.

Mac moved directly into his path, blocking Sullivan's view of Celia. "I don't know what in the hell is going on between you two…"

Neither did Sullivan. He knew what he wanted, though. Her.

"The family is waiting," Mac said. "Give Celia time alone. Give her space."

She'd had space from him—for years.

But he nodded grimly and turned back toward the main house. Brodie and Davis were both there, glowering. They did that a lot, so their expressions weren't particularly surprising. No one spoke until Sullivan reached the porch steps.

"Want to tell us," Brodie asked quietly, "just who that pretty redhead is?"

"A client," Sullivan replied, voice curt. That was the story Celia had said to give, but…*but she flinched when I told her my family never knew about the marriage*. He hadn't told them because talking about Celia had just hurt too much.

From the corner of his eye, he saw the swift glance that Mac gave him, but his brother didn't call him a liar.

"And why is your client…I mean, *our* client," Brodie amended, "walking around the ranch on her own?"

"Because Celia needed a safe place to crash," Mac quickly told him. "And we knew she'd be safe here."

Unable to help himself, Sullivan's gaze once more sought out Celia. The sun was hitting her red hair, bringing out the fire there. She was so achingly beautiful to him. Even more than she'd been years before.

Would he ever look at her and not crave?

No.

Sullivan cleared his throat and tried to focus on his brothers. "I've got news on our mother."

"The rest of the family is waiting inside," Brodie said. "I gathered them all when I got the call from Mac."

Davis was silent. Silent and staring after Celia. There was curiosity in his expression and…suspicion.

"You got a problem?" Sullivan snapped at his brother.

Davis slowly turned his head toward Sullivan. "She seems familiar to me."

"I don't know why she would. I doubt you've ever met." But…uncertainty stirred though him. Many SAD operatives came from military backgrounds. Only Mac knew that he'd committed to that unit. Secrecy had been required, but…

What if Davis was involved with SAD, too? What if Sullivan wasn't the only one keeping secrets?

"Ava and the others are waiting inside," Brodie said. "Don't you think they've waited long enough?"

Sullivan nodded and climbed up the steps. But at the threshold to the ranch house, he hesitated and glanced over his shoulder. Celia had paced toward the bluff. The wind tossed her hair.

I have waited long enough for the thing I want most.

CELIA PULLED OUT her burner phone. She dialed the contact number for her ex-boss, her fingers moving quickly, without hesitation. She'd have to make the call quick because she knew exactly what sort of technology was out there. She couldn't risk someone triangulating the signal from the phone and coming after her.

But she also needed answers.

The phone was answered on the second ring.

"You've got the wrong number," a gruff voice said instantly.

"No," she replied, "I don't."

"Celia?"

"Hello, Ronald." Ronald Worth had been her supervisor at the agency from the first moment she walked through those gleaming doors. He'd weathered many storms with her and she'd certainly never expected this, not from him. "Want to tell me why I'm on the kill list?"

"Celia, where are you?" A heated intensity filled his words. She could picture him in her mind. He'd be in his office, hunched behind his desk, his brow furrowed as he stroked his chin.

"I'm on the run—where else would I be? I mean, when another agent comes gunning for me, it certainly becomes obvious that I'm not exactly on the team's roster any longer."

And if she was being targeted by her own agency, there was only one man who could have ordered that hit. The man she was speaking with right now.

"You aren't on any kill list!" Ronald blasted. "Celia, you said you wanted out, so I started the paperwork for you. New name, new place. You know how the deal works."

Yes, she did. She also knew how things worked when agents were being eliminated and not retired. "I didn't sell secrets. I never turned on anyone."

"Celia, I swear…we aren't after you!"

"Then why is Porter Vance hunting me?"

Silence.

She only had a few more minutes. There was no time to waste with silence. "I've known for a while that something was going on," she continued, her voice stark. "My computer files were hacked. My home— I could tell when someone had broken in." And she'd tried to figure out who was after her. But then things had changed… Mac had called her in to help him on the case in North Dakota, and Sullivan had come back into her life.

And my life imploded.

"I'm being targeted by my own team. After all my years of sacrifice. After all the work I did for you… *why?*" She deserved an answer.

"I'm on your side," Ronald said. "Believe me. Trust me."

She laughed.

"We have to meet, Celia. There are things going on that you don't understand. When you hooked up with the McGuires again, you set off a chain reaction…"

"And you knew all about me hooking up with them?" That would explain Porter's presence at McGuire Securities. Ronald had sent him after her. And Porter had just waited to attack, like the good killer he was.

Is that all any of us are? Good killers?

"I found out something…dammit, I wanted to tell you in person," Ronald groused. "But you didn't come back to the office."

No, she hadn't. Because she'd realized she was being hunted. In their business, when the Agency turned on you, you ran.

A TV show had been made about an agent who was betrayed by his agency. There was a reason that show had been called *Burn Notice*. When the agency decided to target you, then you truly were burned.

"You're still tied to him."

She had no idea what he meant. "This call is over."

"No, wait! Listen, *listen*! You aren't being targeted by the agency. You're being targeted because of your connection to Sullivan McGuire."

She hesitated. It was a trick. It had to be. All signs pointed to the threat coming from the CIA, but...

Maybe Porter was at McGuire Securities because of Sullivan?

No, no, that—

"I didn't want to say this on the phone, but—you're still married to him, Celia."

That wasn't possible. She'd signed papers. Talked to a judge and—

"The divorce wasn't legit. You're still his wife. The man has powerful enemies. You *know* that. Enemies that would do anything to control him. To stop his investigation into his parents' murder. They're trying to send a message to him by hurting you. That's why you've been targeted. That's why your files were hacked. Yeah, yeah, I found out about all that—not because I'm the one doing it, but because I'm trying to protect you."

"This call is over," she said again, because too much time had passed. She didn't want to give away her location.

"If Porter Vance is after you, I didn't send him! He's a free agent now. He's—"

"Dead," she said flatly.

"What?"

"Goodbye, Ronald."

"Celia, wait, you need—"

She hung up. Right now she had no idea what she needed.

SULLIVAN OPENED THE white envelope Celia had given to him. He took out the papers inside and unfolded them.

Around him, his family waited. His brothers and the women they loved.

His sister, Ava, stood a few feet away, with her husband, Mark Montgomery, at her side.

They'd all been waiting so long to unravel the past.

And all Sullivan could think about in that moment was Celia. *I keep hurting her.*

"Damn, man," Mac snapped. "Cut the suspense and just tell us. Why did Mom go into the Witness Protection Program? What happened to her?"

He looked at the pages before him. "It's her death certificate." His eyes narrowed. "The woman she'd been before...they said she was dead. There was never going to be any going back for her." Which was damn odd. Normally, a person in Witness Protection would go back to testify in a trial or—

"She had to get away," Ava said. "She was running when she came here."

They all knew that already.

"Then she met Dad." Grant's voice was solemn. "She never seemed scared to me. My whole life, Mom just seemed...happy."

"She was." Sullivan would never believe otherwise. He'd seen the love and joy in his mother's eyes. He moved the death certificate and focused on the next form that Celia had given him.

A police report. Very old, from the looks of it. Not a

copy. Hell, an original? How had she gotten her hands on that? "Mom saw a murder," he said. No, not a murder, Sullivan realized as he read the paperwork. "An execution. She witnessed a white male in his early twenties walk up and put a gun to the back of her boyfriend's head. The attacker fired one shot, and her boyfriend fell right there." He didn't share the other parts, not right then, but the police reports covered the fact that blood spatter had been all over their mother. That she'd been hysterical at the scene. "According to her statement, the killer said if she talked, he'd come back and shoot her."

And she had been shot, years later. Killed in her own home.

"She talked," Grant said.

Obviously. "It says, 'I won't be afraid.'" He was thumbing through the small stack of papers now. "That's in her handwriting. She wrote out her statement and signed it. She wasn't going to be afraid. She wanted that man brought to justice. A white male with golden eyes. Six foot two. Two hundred pounds." He read the description, aware that his voice had gone flat. All those details were there, stark but not cold—they couldn't be cold when they were written in his mother's hand.

Mac cleared his throat. "She always told us how important it was to help others."

"Especially those who were weaker," Grant added. "Mom never was the type to stand by and let anyone else suffer."

Sullivan's head lifted. He glanced around the room and saw that silent tears had slid down Ava's cheeks.

"There's more, isn't there?" Ava asked, catching his gaze. "Tell us everything now, Sullivan. That's why we're all here."

His gaze swept over them. Grant's wife, Scarlett, was at his side. Their hands were linked. Sullivan stared at their hands for a moment. Grant and Scarlett hadn't been through an easy time. It had taken Grant years to win a place at her side again. If Grant had given up, his brother would have been lost. Sullivan knew that with certainty.

Over the years, Sullivan had carried secrets for Scarlett. He hadn't told his brother about the baby she'd lost because he hadn't wanted to hurt Grant. But those secrets—they *had* hurt. Because Grant had wanted to know everything about Scarlett. He'd wanted to be there for her, through the good and the bad.

Now they were together.

And Grant was frowning at him. "Sully? What is it?"

He shook his head, and his gaze kept sliding over the group. Ava and Mark, Grant and Scarlett, Mac and his pretty Elizabeth. They were all so settled now.

Even the twins had left their wild times behind. Brodie had his hand wrapped around Jennifer's shoulder. Ah, Jennifer…now, there was another woman who understood all about secrets. She'd been hiding the truth about herself from Brodie from the moment that they first met. But when danger had closed in on her, she'd turned to Brodie. She'd trusted him fully.

And Brodie had been willing to walk through hell to keep her safe.

Even Davis and his new wife, Jamie…they'd had to battle a dark past. Jamie had also been in Witness Protection—it was through her that they'd first learned about their mother. But Davis hadn't cared at all about Jamie's past. In fact, he'd been determined to battle the demons that haunted her.

"Secrets," Sullivan muttered. "That's what's been in my way all along."

Grant stepped toward him. "What aren't you telling us?"

He looked back down at the papers. "The cops thought they were after a professional hitter. They figured he'd been hired just to kill Mom's boyfriend. The boyfriend—Henry Jones—was a marine, just back from deployment."

And he remembered right then the way his mother had looked when she first saw him in his uniform. Her lips had trembled. She'd hugged him so tightly.

He had to force his fingers to stay loose around those papers. It took all his strength not to crumple them right then and there. "The marine was gunned right down and Mom was just collateral damage." *The hell she was.* "She wasn't a target, so the gunman let her go. But she went to the authorities. She didn't let fear stop her."

"Did they ever catch the guy?" Jennifer wanted to know. Yes, that would be Jennifer. Wanting to make sure that justice had been served.

"It doesn't say that they did." He'd ask Celia if she knew. "But it does say…the cops suspected this guy was tied to other crimes. Other military personnel who'd been killed." *Executed.* "She was sent away because they believed she would be murdered because she'd come forward. They wanted her to be protected at all costs."

So she'd left her life behind. Gone to Texas.

And started a family there.

A family that hadn't known about her secrets. But…

Dad knew.

He must have known.

"This doesn't make sense to me," Ava said. "Mom

was shot *first*. The men who came after them were trying to make Dad talk, not her. They killed her outright. If those men were here because of her, then what secrets did they think our father knew?" She surged forward. "I remember what he said at the end. Those words have haunted me for years—'I'll never tell you. No matter what you do, I'll never tell you.'" Her voice had gone hoarse with pain. "If the men who killed them were here because of Mom's past, then why would they be trying to make Dad talk? It doesn't make sense, it—"

"He was her handler," Sullivan said, revealing the very last bit of information that Celia had provided in that envelope.

Ava stilled. "What?"

"Mom and Dad didn't meet by chance. When she entered the Witness Protection Program, he was the one who was protecting her. He was the one who was supposed to give her a new start and then, once she was settled, walk away."

"What the hell?" Davis demanded, his expression shocked. "You're saying Dad was law enforcement? I thought—he was always a rancher."

Not always. "I'm not saying it." He gave the papers to his brother. "It's what Celia found out."

Davis blinked. "Back to her, huh? I thought she was a client."

Mac thrust back his shoulders. "A client who helped us. This whole family owes her more than we can ever repay."

Elizabeth gave a quick nod. "I certainly do. If it weren't for Celia, I'd still be running from my past."

Instead, she had a future. Mac had a future.

What do I have?

Papers tied to his bloody past.

"If this Celia might know more, then she needs to come in here," Davis said. His gaze held Sullivan's. "Bring her in with the family."

He wanted to do it, more than anything else. But she'd asked to be kept separate. No…she'd asked after he'd admitted that his family didn't know about her.

Tell them I'm a client.

He glanced toward the door. Was she still at the bluff? That was his favorite spot, and his chest felt tight as he imagined her there.

She had no reason in the world to help him, yet she'd brought him all this information on his family. Why? He had to know.

He turned for the door.

"Bring her in," Davis called again. "Don't you think it's past time we all met her?"

Something about the way Davis said that… Sullivan looked back.

Grant had moved to Davis's side. Grant. The eldest brother. The one who'd worked so hard to hold them all together after they buried their parents.

Grant was staring at him with suspicious eyes. "More secrets, Sully?"

Dammit… "Yes."

"Secrets can destroy you, if you let them," Grant said.

He wasn't in the mood to be destroyed.

He yanked open the door and marched back outside. His gaze swept the area, and, sure enough, Celia was still near the bluff. Her hair was blowing in the faint breeze. The sun warmed her skin, and as he hurried toward her, she turned to face him.

He saw the fear flash across her delicate features. She tried to school her expression, but it was too late.

"What's wrong?" Sullivan demanded instantly as his muscles hardened. He scanned the area, searching for danger, but no one else was there. Just him.

Just her.

Surely she wasn't afraid of him, was she?

Her right hand gripped the burner phone she'd purchased.

"Did you find out something else?" Sullivan asked her.

Celia's lips parted, but then she shook her head. "Nothing that can help us."

"You checked in with your supervisor at the agency, didn't you?" He remembered the guy. Ronald Worth. A by-the-book fellow who'd believed in running a tight ship. Until that ship exploded in his face.

"He says that I'm not on any agent termination list. Ronald swears the threat isn't coming from the agency."

"Then who's targeting you?"

She turned back to face the lake. "It's really beautiful. I mean, I knew the lake was here. It was on the mapping schematics I retrieved, but seeing it in person is something else entirely."

"You got schematics of the ranch property?"

She nodded. "I knew the one thing you wanted most was to find out who killed your parents. And I wanted to give that to you. So I dug…and I bartered and I traded my way to information." She tipped back her head and closed her eyes. "Sometimes, I feel like I know your world so well, but then other times, I realize how much of a stranger you are to me."

She was confusing him. Typical Celia. She'd always been a puzzle he couldn't figure out.

"Why would you want to help me?"

Her lips curved into a smile. "That's something you'll have to figure out on your own."

"Celia…" He heard a door slam. Sullivan glanced over his shoulder and saw that Davis had followed him outside. Seriously, his brother needed to back off. Jaw locking, Sullivan focused on Celia again. Her eyes were still closed, as if she'd shut out the world.

Or maybe just him.

"Do you know my brother Davis?"

"No."

"Are you sure, Celia? He thinks you look familiar to him."

And her eyes opened. She cocked her head as she studied him. "Are you asking if I tried to recruit your brother?"

"Yes."

She shook her head. "I've never met Davis. Just you and Mac. You're the only two McGuires I know."

He could practically feel his brother closing in on him. "Well, you're about to meet Davis. You're about to meet them all."

"No, I told you, I'd stay in the guesthouse and—"

"Are you ever bringing her inside, Sully?" Davis asked as he closed in on them.

Celia blinked and—just that fast—her expression was a perfect blank. Almost like a doll's mask. He didn't like that. He wanted to see her emotions, the good and the bad. Sullivan didn't want Celia to ever hide from him again.

He moved his body, taking up a protective position

in front of her. If she didn't want to face his family, he'd make sure they backed off until she was ready for them.

"You have answers that we need, ma'am," Davis said, his voice softer, gentler. Never let it be said that Davis didn't know how to manipulate and charm in order to get what he wanted. Because gentle? That was the last thing Davis actually was. "So why don't you come inside so we can all talk?"

"She doesn't want to come inside," Sullivan gritted out. "I'm taking her to the guesthouse. I'll discuss the situation more with Celia when we're alone and see what she—"

"Why does that happen?" Davis asked, cutting him off.

Guarded now, Sullivan said, "What?"

"When you say her name, your face changes. So does your voice."

Hell. Davis always had been far too observant.

Davis put his hands on his hips and rocked back on his heels. "You're not a client, are you?"

Celia stepped around Sullivan. "If Sully told you I'm a client, then that's exactly what I am."

Davis smiled. It wasn't an overly friendly sight. Typical Davis. "I've seen you before."

"No," Celia said with certainty. "You haven't. We've never met."

Davis lifted one dark eyebrow. "I never said we'd met. Just that I'd seen you before." He cocked his head as his gaze swept over her. "But your hair was a different color then. Darker, almost black, if I remember correctly."

Sullivan's guts knotted. "Davis…" With that growl, he tried to warn his brother to shut the hell up.

Davis decided to ignore his warning. "I first saw

your photo when I helped Sullivan move into his place. He didn't want to stay here, you see, too many bad memories." He glanced around the ranch. "For a while, all anyone saw was the blood and the death, so I understood that he wanted to leave."

Celia's expression gave nothing away.

"He had a framed photo of you." Davis shook his head. "Crazy thing is...I could have sworn you two were in some kind of chapel."

"You never said a word to me," Sullivan snapped. If the guy had seen the photo, why not question him?

Davis just shrugged. "I figured if you wanted me to know, you'd tell me. But you never did. The years passed, and instead of talking to me, you kept your secrets." He advanced toward Sullivan. "And you started to change. You shut yourself down. I can still remember when you'd laugh freely. When you'd look at the world without suspicion in your eyes." His hand clapped down on Sullivan's shoulder. "With every day that passed, you just pulled away more and more." His hold tightened. "Are you coming back now? Since *she's* here, are you coming back?"

And Sullivan didn't know what the hell he was supposed to say.

Chapter Five

He had her picture.

Celia was pretty much floored by that revelation. A man wouldn't keep a woman's picture, not unless she mattered, right? And she did vaguely remember someone snapping a photo of them at the chapel in Vegas. She'd been so excited then, nearly delirious with happiness for the first time in her life, so she hadn't even stopped to wonder what happened to that image.

Now she knew. Sullivan had kept it.

He stood toe-to-toe with his brother. There was so much tension in the air. She wanted to back away from them, but she couldn't. Celia felt glued to Sullivan's side. No, more than that—she felt protective. It was obvious Davis realized Sullivan had been keeping secrets, but he didn't know the hell Sullivan had endured when he was taken captive. Sullivan had shouldered that burden.

She cleared her throat, wanting to draw Davis's attention away from Sullivan. "I'm Celia James," she said, and offered her hand.

His head turned toward her. His eyes were just as green and just as hard as Sullivan's. "Are you?" His hand curled around hers and she felt the hard press of his calluses against her skin. "Or are you Celia McGuire?"

According to Ronald, I am Celia McGuire. But he had to be wrong. And she wasn't about to talk about that news, not right now. That particular bombshell would wait to be dropped—once she found out whether or not it was even true.

"Celia James," she said again, flatly. "Sullivan and I are divorced." *Are we?* She pulled her hand away from his. "And I am a client. Sullivan agreed to help me. It was one of those I-scratch-your-back—"

"You-scratch-mine deals," Davis finished as his lips quirked. "Right." He paused. "I'm supposed to believe that's the reason you delivered all that intel to him? Because you wanted to pay for his security services?"

"Well…" She slanted a quick sideways glance at Sullivan. The guy appeared to have frozen—or turned to stone. His expression was hard and deadly…and a bit scary. She was afraid that he'd be unleashing on his brother any moment, and that couldn't happen. "McGuire Securities does have a top-notch reputation," Celia replied coolly. "If you want the best, you have to pay for it. By any means necessary."

Davis didn't appear convinced. "And just how is it that you came into possession of such hard-to-acquire material? Because my family has been digging for years, and we couldn't unearth that particular intel."

"I knew where to look," she said carelessly, as if all the hours and bribes and deals she'd made to uncover the past had been easy. A real walk in the park on a Sunday afternoon.

Bull. It had taken blood, sweat and some serious pay-offs to get that information. But she'd been determined.

She hadn't intended to stop, not until she gave Sullivan what he needed. Because she'd thought that maybe then her guilt would end.

"You knew where to look…" Davis laughed. "I sure get the feeling there is a whole lot more to you than meets the eye."

She knew the other McGuires would grill her when she walked into that house. But she'd wear her mask. She'd control the information she revealed to them. There was no need for them to know—

"It was a chapel," Sullivan said, his voice deep and rumbling. "And I still have that picture of her."

What? Her gaze flew to him.

Sullivan's glittering stare was locked on her. "If you'd looked inside my nightstand drawer, you would have found it, Celia."

She shook her head.

"I guess I had a hard time letting go." His hand rose and his fingers skimmed down her cheek. "I tried. You think I don't know how damaged I am? When the chips were down, I was the one who turned on you."

He wasn't saying these things to her. He couldn't be.

"I didn't deserve you. I woke up in that hospital, and I knew that truth. I had been ready to believe the worst of you, when I should have been the one protecting you with every breath that I had."

"Sullivan?"

He looked at his brother. Davis was watching them with an avid gaze. "I married her," Sullivan said to him. "She divorced my fool self. There, happy?"

You're still married to him. Ronald's words rang in her ears.

"And you're right, bro, I did change," Sullivan continued. "Because every single day that passed, I missed her. I wanted her. But she was in the wind and I couldn't find her, not at first. I tried at the agency, but they stone-walled me."

"Uh, the agency?" Davis asked.

But Sullivan just kept going. "I didn't know that Mac had managed to make contact with her—hell, when he first told me about her, that she was going to help us out with that mess that nearly destroyed Elizabeth, I think I went a little crazy."

Her cheeks flashed hot, then ice-cold.

"She's not just a client," Sullivan said as his fingers stroked her cheek once more. "She's always been so much more."

"What are you doing?" Celia whispered to him. "Stop!"

But it was too late.

"I won't ever deny you again," Sullivan swore. "I'll prove that you can trust me."

This wasn't happening.

Frantic, she glanced at Davis. A faint smile curved his lips. A rather satisfied smile. Had he deliberately been pushing Sullivan?

Davis turned away. Took a step. Then stopped. "You talk in your sleep, Sully."

Yes, he did. She'd learned that fact for herself.

"I heard you call for her once. It was easy to put the pieces together after that." Davis looked over his shoulder. "I'll take care of the folks inside. You two need to talk this out before you see the others. If you want to tell the rest of them, do it. For my two cents…you should. But if you want to keep your secrets well, hell, it sure seems like this family was built on them, doesn't it?" Then he walked away.

Celia didn't speak, mostly because she was trying to figure out what to say. Sullivan's hand had fallen away from her cheek, and she felt strangely cold without his touch.

But then, she'd felt a bit cold without him for a very long time.

Don't make the same mistakes. Don't give in to the need. But it was so hard. Especially with him standing right there and—

"You kept my picture?" She hadn't meant to blurt out that question.

He nodded.

"You were the one who told me to walk away." As if she'd ever forget that phone call. "You, Sully, not me."

"You think I don't know what a mistake I made? I was half out of my mind with painkillers. They'd sliced me open in that pit. I thought I was going to die there, and yeah, it was in that hell that I made my mistake. It was there I turned on *you*." He heaved out a breath. "I believed them when they said you'd set me up. They knew so much about my family—things I'd only told you. They knew, C, and rage took over. I wanted—"

He looked away.

"You wanted me to suffer." She wrapped her arms around her stomach and backed up.

"No." His gaze flew right back to her. "I just wanted my life back. I wanted to feel like my heart hadn't been ripped apart. Thinking you'd betrayed me? It gutted me. I was broken. Not by those jerks and their torture, but by what I thought you'd done. I couldn't live like that. I had to get away."

From me.

She focused on breathing, nice and slow.

"Mac told me that you helped him. I didn't know you were driving the damn getaway car—not until you told me. I didn't know you walked into hell for me."

Her lips trembled a bit as she told him, "My boss didn't authorize a retrieval mission for you. It was believed that you were part of the compromised group."

"What?"

Ah, so she had managed to surprise him.

"I was informed you were one of the traitors. That you'd turned on us. Retrieval wasn't an option." Ronald had told her that with sympathy in his voice. "I was boarding the plane to rendezvous with you when my boss gave me the news. The mission had gone to hell. You'd turned. Most of the team members who'd been on-site with you were dead." She'd grabbed the railing beside her and held on tight, not wanting Ronald to see that her legs had nearly collapsed beneath her. "I didn't follow his orders. I contacted Mac instead. We got you out."

He yanked a hand through his hair. "Because you never gave up on me."

"Because it was my fault you'd been taken." Why hide anymore? Davis had gone back into the house. It was just the two of them in that moment, alone on that bluff. No one could hear their secrets. "I was the one who recruited you. I was the one who gave you initial training. I was the one who should've had your back." *Because I was the one who loved you.* "Traitor or not, I was going to find you. You deserved that from me."

His hand fell. "And you deserved a hell of a lot more from me."

"We moved too fast back then," she said, the memories stirring within her. "We barely knew each other. When the chips were down, what more could we expect?"

He stepped closer to her. "More. Expect one hell of a lot more from me this time." His arms wrapped around her and he pulled her close.

She should step away. She should stop him.

Instead, Celia rose onto her toes. She locked her hands around his shoulders, and when his head lowered toward her, she kissed him.

MAC WAS WAITING for Davis just inside the house. When he saw Davis's expression, he demanded, "What did you do?" Trust Davis to go meddling.

Davis shut the door. "You and Sully…did you really think I didn't know what the hell was going on? He vanished for weeks, and when he came back, he was as pale as a ghost. I knew my brother had been hurt." He rolled back his shoulders. "I just respected him enough not to beat him while he was down and demand answers."

"You think you have those answers now?" Mac kept his voice low. Davis might be in the know, but the rest of the family wasn't, not yet.

"I have some answers, but definitely not all. I knew when I saw them together that she was the one who tied him in knots. His obsession, come to life."

Mac exhaled. "Davis, it's not that easy. You don't know her…"

"She's Celia James. I just shook her hand."

Mac glared at the guy. Davis put his palms up. "Look, I know what matters, okay? I know that Sully lights up when he's near her."

But did he know how much pain Sully had brought her before? How much pain Sully had brought himself? "She's already got a dead body in her wake. Danger follows her." Mac liked Celia. He respected her. But that didn't mean he wasn't aware of the risk that she presented—to Sullivan and to them all. "That dead body that was found outside McGuire Securities last night? Celia knew the guy. Sully and I think he was trying to kill her."

A faint furrow appeared between Davis's eyebrows, the only sign of his concern. "Yet he wound up dead." A brief hesitation. "By her hand?"

"Celia said she didn't kill him."

"Do you believe her?"

"I want to." He truly did. But he couldn't trust her with his family's lives. "But I haven't ever been that close to her."

"Not like Sully," Davis murmured. "He got close enough to marry her..."

But he still didn't fully trust her. And that had been their downfall.

"Sully mentioned the agency a few moments ago," Davis said.

Mac hid his surprise. Davis was obviously probing, but Mac just stared back at his brother.

"If overseas work was involved, and I'll assume it was with Sullivan's background..." Davis cocked his head to the right "...then the agency, I'm guessing, is... CIA?"

"If you say so."

Davis grunted. "You *and* Sully, huh? Because you know her well, too. Was she your handler?"

Mac shrugged.

Davis's eyes hardened. "You never told me you were an operative."

"I don't remember you asking." Mac rubbed his jaw, feeling the scrape of stubble there. He considered stone-walling his brother, but decided that enough was damn enough. "Someone had to watch Sully's back."

"I think that's what Celia's doing."

No, he rather thought Celia and Sully were doing something else entirely. Especially if he knew his brother…

"But now that I know we're dealing with the CIA," Davis added, "I know which contacts to use in order to check her out."

Right. Because Davis would never accept Celia at face value. He never accepted anyone at face value. Their whole family had trust issues.

"Let's just see what my sources have to say about her…"

"Your sources?" Mac pushed. Since when did Davis have sources at the CIA?

Davis smiled at him. "You think you and Sully were the only ones approached by the CIA? Get in line, bro. I didn't take them up on the offer, but that doesn't mean my friends didn't."

Hell. He'd wondered about that… Davis and Brodie had both been SEALs, and SEALs would have made perfect candidates for the CIA's Special Activities Division. With their elite training, they would have been perfect agent picks for the covert operations.

"Give me thirty minutes," Davis said with a nod, "and I'll know everything I need to know about Celia James…"

"Good luck with that," Mac told him. *Because you'll need it.*

Thirty minutes wouldn't be nearly long enough to explore the mystery that was Celia. Sully could have easily told the guy that fact.

CELIA WAS IN his arms. She was kissing him. She tasted sweeter than candy, better than wine, and he never wanted to let her go.

And I won't.

Not this time.

Sullivan pulled her closer. Kissed her deeper. He loved it when she gave that faint moan for him. He could feel the tips of her breasts pushing against him. Perfect breasts. They'd always fit just right in his hands. He wanted to strip her. To taste every delectable inch of her body.

When the pleasure swept over her, Celia was so beautiful.

She's always beautiful.

His hands slid down her back. Moved to the curve of her hips. She had such a fine—

Celia pushed against him.

Jaw locking, Sullivan eased back, but he didn't release his hold on her.

"Tell me what you want from me." Her voice had gone husky with desire.

What he wanted? Easy. Everything. But he said, "From now on, no secrets."

Her eyelashes flickered.

"I won't keep any secrets from you," he promised her. "So what I want right now, more than anything… is you. I want to take you someplace private, where I don't have to worry about my family intruding on us. I want to strip you, and I want to drive you wild."

That plan seemed simple enough to him.

"But what do *you* want?" Sullivan asked her. "Tell me, and I'll make it happen."

Her gaze searched his. The desire was plain to see in her stare. Her cheeks had flushed and her lips were red, slightly swollen, from his mouth. Sexy as all hell.

"I want you," she said slowly. "I don't want any hesitations. I want us, alone, and I want to let go of every fear that I've ever had."

Yes.

He caught her hand in his and pretty much started pulling her toward the guesthouse.

Only…

A glance toward the main ranch house showed him that Mac was on the porch. The guy jumped off the steps and headed toward him.

No, no, no. His brother could not really have timing that bad. It just couldn't be possible. "See…" Sullivan sighed. "There's the family, intruding."

Mac kept marching toward them. The guy was totally ignoring Sullivan's get-away glare. "They want to meet her," Mac called.

And I want to keep her all to myself. That equaled a problem in his book.

"She brought them answers," Mac continued as he sauntered closer. "Well, answers and more questions… They're all waiting inside for her."

So much for Davis taking care of them. Just where had his other brother gone?

Celia bit her lower lip. A shudder of need rushed

through him. He wanted to have that lip against his mouth again. He wanted to taste her, and if she wanted to bite him…*feel free, baby*.

The sex between them had always been intense. Wild.

Hot.

His arousal shoved against the front of his jeans, and the last thing he wanted was a sit-down with his family. He'd been away from Celia too long. She'd just admitted that she wanted to be with him, too.

Now…this?

Fate was so cruel. Terribly, twistedly cruel.

"I don't have any more answers to give them," Celia said. "Everything that I had…I gave that to Sully. There wasn't any more for me to find on your mother. I looked. I searched. But I couldn't find more. I think there was another file on the man who shot her boyfriend. She went back in for a sit-down with the local cops, but that file was destroyed in a fire. And the cops she talked with back then? They both died in a shoot-out a few months later. So if she ever officially said anything else about the man who executed Henry Jones, no record exists of that testimony."

"Come inside," Mac said with a slow nod. "It's time, Celia."

Time? A swift glance at Mac showed that his expression had turned very solemn. Sullivan realized this wasn't just about the past—it was about the present that Mac knew Sullivan wanted with Celia.

She nodded. "Fine. We'll be right behind you."

Mac turned and headed back to the house.

Celia watched him in silence, and she made no move

to follow. Sullivan started to feel…nervous, and that sure wasn't something he was used to experiencing.

"I'm scared," she finally admitted.

Nothing she could have confessed would have shocked him more.

"What if they don't…what if they don't like me?"

His jaw nearly hit the ground at that whispered question. Then he laughed.

Celia blushed furiously when she saw his expression.

"Oh, baby, no, I'm sorry." He pulled her close once more. If he had his way, she'd always be close to him. "I wasn't laughing at you." He'd never do that. "I was laughing because…you've faced down killers. International terrorists. And you're worried about what my family thinks of you?"

"Yes." Still flushing, she held his gaze. "I am."

She shouldn't be. "I'm just hoping they don't say something that sends you running," he said honestly. "They can be overwhelming." To say the least.

"I've never had a family, Sullivan. You know I was raised in the foster system."

Yes, he remembered her telling him that. And he remembered thinking, *I'll be your family, baby*. He still wanted to offer her a family. A home. All that she'd ever dreamed of.

"I was pretty much on my own for as long as I can remember." She cast a quick glance toward the house. "There were no big holidays. No family gatherings. No barbecues in the summer. A crowd like that one in there—all the emotions—it just…what if I say the wrong thing?"

"You won't." He was dead certain. "Elizabeth is already eternally grateful to you. Mac is ready to slay any dragon that appears…and you have me."

"Do I?"

"Yes." *For as long as you want me.* "We've got this."

She smiled and her dimples flashed. He actually felt his heart stop at the sight of those dimples. It was a real smile from her. Not cold or taunting. Not a fake stretch of her lips. Her dimples winked. Her eyes gleamed.

In that instant, she was once again the woman he'd married.

"Let's do this," Celia said. Her fingers twined with his. They headed toward the house. They didn't speak again as they climbed the porch steps and walked inside.

But as soon as they crossed the threshold, every bit of conversation in the house died. All eyes turned on them.

Not so subtly, Sullivan moved closer to Celia. If anyone so much as looked sideways at her…

Ava rushed forward. She shoved Sullivan to the side and threw her arms around Celia. "Thank you," Sullivan heard his sister gasp out.

Over Ava's shoulder, Celia stared at Sullivan with wide eyes. *What do I do?* She mouthed those words to him, looking rather like a gorgeous deer in the headlights.

But before Sullivan could say anything, Ava was talking again. She pulled back a bit but didn't let Celia go. "This is a huge break for us. Knowing more about our mother *and* our father—it's a game changer!" She shook her head. "I don't know how you got that intel, but thank you. I am in your debt and I will do anything—"

"No." Celia's voice was quiet, but very firm. "You don't owe me anything, I promise you that."

Ava finally let Celia go. Her husband, Mark, who

had a habit of staying protectively close to Ava, came to her side.

Celia squared her shoulders and peered at the assembled crowd, and it truly was quite a big group. Sullivan looked at them all, trying to see them from a stranger's perspective. He and his brothers all looked alike—dark hair, green eyes. Tall and strong. Ava—she had long, dark hair and the McGuire eyes—but she was delicate. Physically, anyway. Inside, the woman had the heart of a lion.

The other women there were all beauties in their own way. Beauties and true forces to be reckoned with. They'd each had a time battling to save the men they loved. Nothing had stopped them in their fight.

Jennifer was sleek and polished. Scarlett was glowing, her hair hanging over her shoulder in a braid. Elizabeth was wearing jeans and a loose T-shirt. Her smile for Celia was warm and welcoming. And Dr. Jamie, the vet who'd married Davis, brushed off her hands—she'd probably been out working with the animals earlier—made her way to Celia and offered her hand. "It's a pleasure to meet you."

Celia took her hand. She still looked a bit overwhelmed, but she didn't appear ready to bolt. "And it's nice to finally meet all of you."

Did the others note that little slip of *finally*? He was betting some of them did. Celia seemed to catch herself, and then she turned a horrified glance on Sullivan.

He just smiled. "Celia isn't a client."

She still had her spine ramrod straight. Her expression had turned back to that calm mask. She had—

"She's the woman I owe my life to."

Celia shook her head.

But he nodded. "So, yeah, Ava, the family is in her debt. We all owe her." He caught Celia's fingers in his and brought them to his lips. He kissed her knuckles, not caring at all that others would see the move. He *wanted* them to see it. Celia was his, and he was more than ready to fight for her. "But no one owes her more than I do."

"CELIA JAMES IS at the McGuire ranch." After delivering that message, his caller hung up the phone.

The ranch. He should have known. It seemed oddly fitting, as if the journey had come full circle.

Such a bloody start in that place. He'd thought that he was ending a nightmare when he left that ranch. He hadn't realized that the McGuire children would be as much of a nuisance as their parents.

They'd just kept digging.

Why hadn't they let the past die? They could have all moved on. All had a chance at happiness.

But no…they just hadn't stopped. And the trail of bodies had lengthened as the past was unraveled.

Now more would die. The body count would keep coming. It would be tragic. One of those tales that people read about and shook their heads and muttered sadly about what a loss it had all been.

The attack would need to look like an accident, of course. There would be less suspicion that way. A fire would work. Maybe a few well-placed bombs. He knew all about planting explosives. You just had to set your device in the right spot.

And if he moved carefully enough, he could make that happen. He could create a big blaze that would take out the McGuire ranch…and those unlucky enough to be caught inside.

Maybe some would escape. He'd have to be ready for them. Eventually, he'd get them all. It was time to end this story. Time to stop sweating and worrying that the secrets from his past would be uncovered.

He had a job to do, and he'd do it.

The key…the key would be Celia. Celia James. All the intel he'd gathered on her indicated that she'd always been so good at following orders.

Except when it came to Sullivan McGuire.

But everyone had to have a weakness…and for Celia, Sullivan was that weakness.

So does that mean you're his weakness, too?

He was about to find out.

Chapter Six

She pretty much ran into the guesthouse. As soon as Sullivan shut the door behind her, Celia exhaled on a rush of relief before she spun to face him.

Sullivan leaned back against the door. "Was it really that bad?"

No, it hadn't been bad at all. His family had been welcoming. Kind. They'd opened their home and been so *grateful* as they talked to her.

Now that she considered things more…maybe it had been bad. Maybe it had been hell. *Because I wanted to belong there with them.* "You made them think we're still involved."

He shrugged.

And then he yanked his dark T-shirt over his head and tossed it to the floor.

"Sullivan!" His name emerged way huskier than she'd intended. She swallowed and tried again. "What are you doing?"

He quirked an eyebrow at her. "Really, baby? I'm stripping."

He was. His hands were on his belt.

"Why?"

He'd unhooked his belt. "Because I'm going to make love to you."

Her heart pounded against her chest. "Your family—"

"They're not going to bother us. I told them you were up for most of the night. A true story, by the way. And that you needed to crash." He hadn't lowered the zipper. Not yet. He walked to her, those jeans hugging his lean hips. His six-pack abs tempted her far too much. "You can crash with me."

She put up her hands and wound up touching his warm, strong muscles.

"You said you wanted me," he reminded her.

Celia didn't need that reminder. "I never stopped." Did he think that just because they'd been miles apart, he hadn't been in her mind? Her dreams? There had been plenty of fantasies that left her aching for him.

"Baby, I'm pretty sure I'll go insane if I'm not with you now." His eyes darkened as he stared at her. "It's been too long."

Her breath hitched. "But what happens tomorrow?" Were they just going to walk away after this? One night and then goodbye?

"Whatever you want to happen." His head bent as he pulled her toward him. His lips feathered over her neck. Right in that spot that she loved. "Anything you want."

He was what she wanted, and she wouldn't pretend otherwise. Her hands slid over him, moving across those faint scars, but then she pushed against him. There was something she needed to do.

Instantly, he stilled. "Celia?" His head lifted.

She smiled up at him. "I missed you, Sully."

His face softened.

She pressed a kiss to the scar near his heart. He sucked in a sharp breath.

"Baby…"

"Did you miss me?" She kissed another scar, moving down his body. She wanted to kiss every wound that he had. She wished she could take away the pain. Make the past better—for them both.

But she couldn't go back.

Instead, maybe they could go forward, together.

"I missed you more than you'll ever know." His words were rough, almost guttural, and the emotion in them had a surge of warmth spreading through her.

She'd never wanted another man the way she desired him.

Sullivan pushed her to the edge—and beyond.

She kissed another scar. Her knees hit the floor before him as she tried to get closer. The scars—there were so many of them and—

"No." In a flash, he'd lifted her up into his arms. "If you touch me anymore like that, I'm done." His voice made her shiver. "I can't go slowly this time. I have to be in you. I *need* you." He kissed her as he carried her through the house. Deep and hard and hungry, his mouth took hers. She loved his kiss. Celia ached for him.

In moments, they were in a bedroom. They fought with her clothes as they both tried to toss them away. Then she was in just her bra and panties.

He ditched his shoes and dropped his jeans beside the bed. He stood there for an instant, staring at her.

She certainly looked her fill at him. He was heavily aroused, a big, hulking form near the bed. His eyes were so very dark now, the green almost completely gone. A faint red stained his cheeks as he stared at her and asked, "How did you become even more beautiful?"

He'd always made her feel beautiful, when they were in bed together and when they weren't. She lifted her arms toward him.

He touched her, and she was surprised to see that his fingers were shaking. "Sully?"

"I want you so much." His hand fisted. "I don't think I can hold on to my control much longer. I should seduce you, caress every inch of you…"

She rose next to him. Kissed his neck. Licked along the line of his racing pulse. Then she bit him, a light, sensual nip. "You can do all of that," Celia whispered to him, "next time." Her hands slid over his back. "But this time, I don't want to wait, either. I just want you."

He kissed her. Not gently. Not tentatively. Instead, he took her mouth with a wild need that she eagerly met.

His hands slid down her body. He pushed her legs apart and then he was touching her. Sliding his long, broad fingers over her sensitive core. She arched against him even as her nails scraped lightly over his arms. She wasn't looking for seduction. She wanted the wild ride that came with him. The pleasure that swept her away from everything else.

But he'd bent over her and now he took her breast in his mouth. Licking, kissing, driving her crazy even as his wicked fingers kept working the center of her need. Her muscles locked and her breath heaved out. *"Sullivan."*

He moved between her legs. She felt the broad shaft of his arousal pressing against her and she pushed her hips toward him.

"Protection." His hands locked around her hips. "Baby, I'm sorry, I didn't bring anything—"

"I'm covered and I'm clean." She didn't want to stop.

His gaze held hers. "I'm clean, too."

Then it would be this way. Flesh to flesh. The way it had been the night they married. The night so much had changed.

Still holding her stare, he sank into her. The pleasure wasn't easy then. *Easy* didn't apply at all. It was as if a volcano went off inside her, and all the desire that she'd held back for so long just exploded. Their bodies moved in perfect tune, a fast, hard rhythm. The bed was squeaking, she was panting and every glide of his body had her wanting more.

Wanting everything.

Deeper. Harder. Faster.

They rolled across the bed and suddenly she was on top of him. His hands locked around her hips as he lifted her, again and again, and the pleasure slammed into her. She could only gasp out his name and hold on tight as the release consumed her.

But Sullivan wasn't done. His grip was steely on her as he surged into her, deeper and ever stronger. She fell down against his chest, kissing him, and he rolled them across the bed once more, maneuvering so that he was deep, so very deep in her core.

When his release hit him, she felt the warmth deep inside and it set her off again, aftershocks that had her shivering and holding tightly to him.

And when it was over, when her heart wasn't racing in her chest any longer, she lifted her lashes and stared into his eyes.

Part of her had wondered if it would still be as good

with him. Maybe she'd turned their past into something more than it had actually been.

But…no.

It was still as good. No, it was even better.

"I missed you," Sullivan confessed as he turned to curl his body around hers.

Her hand lifted and pressed over his heart. *And I missed you.*

How was she supposed to walk away from him again?

THE SUNLIGHT FELL onto the bed, sliding over the red of Celia's hair and turning her skin an even warmer gold.

Sullivan studied her for a moment, his gaze slowly trailing over her face. Her eyes were closed, her full lips parted in the faintest of smiles. Part of him—such a big part—wanted to just stay there with her. To forget everything else.

But…

But someone was trying to kill Celia, and that *wasn't* going down when he was near. He leaned forward and pressed a soft kiss to her temple, and then, moving as quietly as he could, he eased from the bed. Sullivan grabbed his clothes and slipped into the hallway.

He dressed quickly, then left the guesthouse, making sure to secure the place first. The sun seemed too bright outside and every step that he took away from Celia felt wrong.

But he needed to work. He was going to get his brothers to call in every single favor they were owed. Someone had to know something about the person after Celia. Because if it wasn't a hitter from the agency, then just who wanted her dead?

When he strode back into the main house, he saw that the group had disassembled. Only Mac was still there—Mac and Davis. Mac turned toward him and asked, "Did Celia get settled?"

"Ah, yeah, I got her settled right in." He cleared his throat. "She's sleeping now. She didn't get much sleep last night—not with us spending so much time trying to figure out where that shooter had gone." After firing at the medical examiner's office, the fellow had vanished without a trace.

Davis grunted. "Mac was bringing me up to speed on all that happened."

Sullivan lifted an eyebrow. He was sure Davis had been learning plenty. Sullivan crossed his hands over his chest and studied Davis. Of all the brothers, he'd always thought he, Mac and Davis were the most alike—not big on trust, and far too well acquainted with suspicion. "You think I don't know what you did?" Sullivan asked him. "I know, because it's exactly what I would have done, too."

Davis didn't move from his position on the couch. He sprawled there, looking as if he didn't have a care in the world.

"You dug into her background, didn't you?" Sullivan guessed. "Probably as soon as you left us on that bluff."

Davis rolled one shoulder in a careless shrug. "Is it so wrong that I wanted to know a bit about the woman you married?"

Sullivan's back teeth ground together. "We don't need to make her any more of a target, so I'm hoping you used *some* discretion when you started prying."

"Monroe Blake."

The name was familiar, but...

"We were SEALs together, and I happen to know that he joined the Special Activities Division a while back." Davis inclined his head toward Sullivan while Mac just watched in silence. "I called Monroe because I wanted someone else's take on your lady. No offense, but you're not exactly unbiased in this situation."

"I sure as hell hope you can trust the guy..."

"I saved Monroe's hide a time or ten, so he owed me."

Owing someone didn't equal trust.

"And he saved me," Davis added quietly. "When he should have just hauled butt and gotten out of there. He walked through the fire for me." His voice was flat. "So, yes, I trust him."

Sullivan's shoulders relaxed a bit at that revelation. "And what did he have to say?"

"A guy named Ronald Worth is in charge of the division."

Yeah, he already knew that. Ronald had been there during Sullivan's unfortunate employment. All hell had broken loose, and he'd rather thought that Ronald would go down with the ship. He hadn't. Obviously, it paid to have friends in high places.

"According to Monroe, Ronald had been grooming your Celia to be his replacement. She was the shining protégée who was supposed to take over when he retired."

Your Celia. He wanted her to be his again.

"Only Celia seems to be gone out on some kind of mission right now, or at least, that's what good old Ronald is telling the others."

"And your contact didn't have any qualms about

sharing this information with you?" Suspicion pushed inside him.

"I didn't ask for her location. I didn't ask him to disclose any top-secret intel. I just asked Monroe for his take on your Celia."

Sullivan waited.

Davis stared back at him.

The guy loved to push buttons. Brothers. They could be such damn pains. "And that take was…?" Not that it mattered. He knew Celia.

"Dedicated. Brutally smart. And willing to go to any extremes to protect her team." Davis scratched his chin. "Though there were some rumors swirling about her when my buddy first joined the division. She'd gone in, risking her life, in order to retrieve an agent suspected of turning on the group. Seems she walked straight into hell."

Sullivan's gaze cut to Mac. "I thought she just drove the getaway car," he gritted out.

Mac shrugged. "Not quite. She was there with me, every step of the way, helping me to battle the men who had you. She's the one who begged you to live when we found you lying so still in that pit, and Celia was the one—standing right there—who heard you say that she was the enemy. That she couldn't be trusted and you never wanted to see her again."

He could hear his own heart pounding. Every breath became painful. "I loved her." He rasped out those words. They were hard to say because he'd held them in for so long. But it was past time for him to admit the truth.

"I fell for her," Sullivan continued quietly. "Hard and way too fast. Love wasn't supposed to be like that.

I wasn't supposed to think about her every moment. I wasn't supposed to need her that much."

A frown had pulled Mac's eyebrows down low.

"I saw Mom and Dad. They loved each other. It wasn't dark and frantic. Their love was steady. Strong." The way he'd thought love should be. "I was out of control with Celia. I hardly recognized myself at all. I couldn't let her go—I wanted to tie her to me in any and every way possible." It had been that way from the beginning. Hell, he hadn't even joined the CIA out of some big desire to help his country. He'd done it *for her.* To be close to Celia.

"So you married her," Mac murmured.

He nodded. "Trust wasn't easy for me. Not with our parents' deaths and then…so much was happening. We weren't getting anywhere with the investigation and I—" He expelled a rough breath. "There were double agents in our group. I was set up. Taken down. My location was known as soon as I stepped foot off that plane. They knew so much about me…"

His gaze slid from Mac to Davis. "About all of you. They taunted me. Said that they'd take me out with a bullet at the end, just the way my parents had gone out. But first, they wanted information. Intel on covert missions I'd worked, that *you'd* all worked. They planned to use me in order to get to all of you."

Davis sighed. "And you thought Celia was the one who'd served you up to them."

"She was supposed to be on that plane with me, but at the last minute the plans were altered. Instead of traveling over with me then, she was coming two days later." Though now he was so grateful for that change.

Because if she'd been taken, too...*would Celia be dead?* "And the other agents—the ones who'd turned—they'd been working with her far longer than I had. She was close to them. They told me...my captors said everything she'd done was part of a setup. Even marrying me was just a ruse so that I'd trust her and be ready to follow any order she gave. Like a lamb to the slaughter."

"And you believed them?" Davis asked quietly.

"Not at first. But when you go days without food or water and the jerks start slicing you open and they keep playing videos...recordings of Celia talking about her plans... Hell, at first, I knew those recordings had to be fake. I knew it. I knew her!" His hands had fisted. "But I went a little crazy after a while. When I was sure no one was coming for me, it got harder to think straight. I was so angry. At the captors. At myself. I wasn't going to turn, no matter what they said, so I had to use that rage to help me stay alive."

Mac rose and came toward him. "You know that's part of the interrogation techniques they use. They want to break you down. Because when you give up your hope, you have nothing left."

Celia was my hope. "I needed her too much," he said again. "I realized that in the pit. The way I felt for her— it scared even me. I didn't think it was normal. I wasn't normal. And when I got out, I still had so much anger in me." Now he would confess his darkest shame. "I was afraid I'd hurt her. I had to send her away from me."

"What?" Davis demanded, voice sharp. "Sullivan, hell, no, you—"

"You didn't see me back then. I stayed away. I thought..." He swallowed the lump in his throat. "I thought they'd succeeded, you see. That they had broken my mind. I was too dark. Too dangerous. The way I felt about Celia…it wasn't safe for me to be near her." Because love could become a dark and twisted obsession. And if he'd ever hurt her…

"Post-traumatic stress," Mac said. "Damn, man, I didn't know it had gotten that bad. You should have told me…"

More like post-traumatic hell. "I crawled my way back." Moment by moment. "But yeah, Davis, to get back to what you said before about me calling for her… I talk in my sleep. I call out for her. I have night terrors and flashbacks and sometimes I wonder if it will ever end." He drew in a shuddering breath. "But I've tried living without her, and it sucks." No other way to describe it. "The need is still there. The yearning for her. Only her. I thought it would go away. It didn't. But *I* have control back. I'm not going to that dark place, ever again. I can be the man she needs."

Mac locked his hand around Sullivan's shoulder. "You should have told me this stuff."

"We all were going through enough…with our parents and Ava." For a while, he'd worried that Ava might hurt herself, too. She'd been in so much pain. "I was just trying to make it through the days and nights." His brothers had said they'd seen him withdrawing. It had been true. He'd had to withdraw in order to survive.

Sullivan shook his head. "That's it. My screwed-up, twisted past." He inclined his head toward a watchful Davis. "I want to be better, for her. I want to be the man she deserves now. She came to me for help, and you can damn well bet that is exactly what I'll give her." He'd give her everything he had.

"So you trust her...completely?"

"Yes." Said with no hesitation. "So even if your contact—"

"Monroe said that he'd only trust a few people to watch his back, and Celia would be at the top of his list."

Sullivan nodded. "And does he know who is after her? Have they recently worked any missions that put a target on her?"

Mac's hand tightened on his shoulder. "Celia didn't tell you that?"

"Celia hasn't told me much at all about her work with the government." Probably because she was protecting the other agents. "She just said she was getting out."

Davis sighed. "If we're going to help her, she'll have to open up about her past, too. You think she'll do that?"

He wasn't sure. And he wasn't going to push her too hard. "She'll share what she can." To him, it was as simple as that. "She'll—"

His phone rang. Frowning, Sullivan pulled the phone from his back pocket. *Unknown caller.* He started to just ignore the call, but a tightness in his gut made him answer. "Sullivan."

"McGuire..." a man's voice drawled. "The deadly ex-marine. It's been too long."

"Who in the hell is this?"

"You aren't doing Celia any favors by staying close to her."

He listened carefully to the caller's voice. Arrogant tone. Faint drawl.

"Do you remember me?" the voice pushed. "Once upon a time, you worked under my command."

The voice finally clicked for him. "Ronald Worth."

He saw surprise flash on Davis's face.

"Celia wouldn't listen to reason, so I hope you will," Ronald said.

It was no surprise that the guy had managed to get his number. The fellow no doubt had plenty of strings he could pull. Accessing a private number would be all too easy for a man like him.

"We need to meet," Ronald said bluntly. "Just the two of us. There's a lot you don't know about, and I don't exactly feel comfortable sharing over the phone."

"Because you think someone could be listening in?"

Ronald laughed. "I don't trust anyone these days. Friends can turn on you in a blink. So can family. But that's a lesson you already learned, isn't it?"

His brothers moved closer as Sullivan swiped the button on his phone to turn on the speaker. "Why do you just want to meet with me?" Sullivan asked. "Why not Celia?"

"Celia has already thrown away her career for you," Ronald said. "Do you really want her to lose her life, too?"

His fingers tightened around that phone. "Did you just threaten her?"

"No, son, I'm the one working desperately to keep her safe. She's got hunters on her trail because she doesn't have agency protection any longer, not officially. What she has…that's me. That woman has been like a daughter to me, and the last thing I want is to see her dead."

"That's the last thing I want, too."

"Then maybe you shouldn't have pushed her to go digging into the past."

Sullivan frowned at that response. He hadn't asked Celia to—

"Now the target isn't just on the McGuires. It's on her."

Suspicion gnawed at Sullivan's gut. There was just something about the guy's voice. "You know who killed our parents, don't you?"

"I know you shouldn't have pulled Celia into this mess."

"You bastard…" Had that man known the truth all along? *"Tell me."*

Fury was marked on Davis's face, too, a fury that matched Sullivan's. If Ronald Worth knew who'd killed their parents, why would he have kept silent for so long? Why not come forward?

"You have no idea the players who are involved in this game," Ronald stated flatly.

"It's not a game. It's our lives."

More laughter. "You think that by keeping Celia at the ranch, you're keeping her safe?"

Ice slid through Sullivan's veins. "How do you know I'm at the ranch?" But hell… "You triangulated the signal, didn't you? Is *that* why you called? To find out where I was?" And he'd just given up the fact that Celia was with him. He should have known—

"I'm not the threat," Ronald snapped. "I'm the one trying to help. Now if you want to learn more, you'll meet me. Just you. Slip away and leave Celia with your brothers. They can keep guard. Come to see me, and I'll tell you everything I know."

"You'll tell me who's after Celia?"

"I'll tell you the names of the men who killed your parents."

Go, Davis mouthed.

Mac nodded grimly.

"Where?" A flat demand from Sullivan.

Ronald rattled off the address.

And that ice just got thicker in Sullivan's veins. "You're already down in Austin?" Where another ex-agent had been killed just hours before? No way was that a coincidence.

"I've been trailing Celia. I lost contact with her after she left North Dakota. She has to come in, before it's too late."

Sullivan was starting to think it already was too late.

"Can you meet me in two hours?" Ronald pressed.

"Yeah, I'll be there."

"Good. Remember, come alone. You're not going to want anyone else to hear this…"

Did the guy think he was a fool?

The call ended.

Sullivan stared at his brothers.

"All right…" Mac sighed. "So what's our plan of attack?"

Chapter Seven

She was alone in the bed. Celia knew she was alone even before she cracked open her eyes. She felt cold, and she knew that Sullivan had left her.

Slowly, she stretched, aware of a few aches and pains in all the right places. She was naked and the sheet slid over her skin as she sat up. The sun still shone brightly through the window, so she knew a lot of time hadn't passed.

I didn't mean to fall asleep. I never fall asleep that way...not with someone so close to me.

But she'd felt safe in Sullivan's arms, and it had seemed so very natural to just close her eyes and drift away.

And just where had Sullivan *drifted* away to? She rose from the bed, pulling the sheet with her. "Sullivan?" Celia called, but he didn't answer her, and it only took a few moments to realize that he'd left the guesthouse. Pursing her lips, she went back to the bedroom. She eyed her clothes, scattered on the floor, then moved to the closet. A search through the boxes in there revealed some old jeans and a T-shirt. Very close to her size, a little too tight in the rear, but they'd work. She figured the clothes must belong to Ava or Jamie.

Now to find some shoes…

A few minutes later, she'd pulled a pair of tennis shoes out from beneath the bed. Those shoes would be so much better than her heels. She'd have to remember to thank those ladies later for the items they'd left behind.

Dressed, she hurried toward the front of the guesthouse. She'd go out, find Sullivan and then…then she had to figure out her next step. She certainly wasn't going to sit back and hide at the ranch. Hiding wasn't her style. Never had been. She'd contact Ronald again and figure out if he was telling the truth about the agency. Maybe…could another traitor have infiltrated their unit? The same way a traitor had gotten inside when Sullivan was taken before?

It was possible, even with all the vigorous screenings that were in place. Some people were so very good at lying.

She opened the door. Hurried outside. She'd turned toward the main house when she saw Sullivan and Mac heading in the direction of the cars. For an instant, she stilled.

No, he wasn't just planning to leave without telling her. Was he?

But Sullivan didn't glance her way. He jumped into the car, his movements too quick and tense. Mac followed, riding shotgun.

Those men needed to think again. She wasn't the left-behind type.

Her pace picked up until she was nearly running. Her instincts were screaming at her.

Sullivan cranked the car.

Oh, no, you don't.

She put herself in front of the vehicle, blocking his path.

Instantly, the engine died and Sullivan jumped from the car. "Celia!" Her name sounded like an angry snarl. Funny, earlier it had sounded like a caress. But that had been when they were in bed together, and obviously those moments had been fleeting. "What in the hell are you doing?" he asked.

"Getting your attention," she answered immediately as she braced her legs apart. "You didn't seem to notice my approach, so before you went roaring out of here, I thought I'd stop you."

"You jumped in front of the car!"

She smiled at him. "There was no jumping. Just step-ping."

"I could have run over you!"

"No."

He gaped at her.

She glared back. "Where are you going?"

Sullivan glanced over his shoulder, looking toward Mac. Mac had climbed out of the car and was watching them with a tense expression.

"I have a meeting," Sullivan said, his voice still gruff. "It shouldn't take too long. I didn't want to disturb you, because I knew you had to be dead on your feet."

As if he wasn't? "Who's this meeting with?"

His lips thinned. A total sign he didn't want to tell her.

"Sullivan?" she prompted.

His hands curled around her shoulders.

As if a little touch from him was going to distract her. "No secrets, remember?"

He swallowed and his Adam's apple clicked. "I remember."

And that's why you were trying to sneak away? The guy had a whole lot to learn about *not* keeping secrets.

"I was told to come alone," he said.

Mac was shotgun. That hardly qualified as alone. She lifted one eyebrow and tried not to tap her foot as she waited.

"Ronald Worth."

Her jaw almost dropped. "My boss? You're going to meet my boss?" Or rather, her ex-boss. Celia's stomach knotted. "Why?" And why wouldn't she be included in that meeting?

"Because he knows who killed my parents. The guy called me. Set up a meeting." He looked at his watch. "I'm supposed to be there—alone—in the next hour."

This wasn't right. And it was making zero sense to her. "How would he know who killed your parents?" When she'd first started digging into Sullivan's past, it had been Ronald who told her there was nothing to find. He'd been the one to say she had to stay out of that old investigation.

Not our area. He'd said that curtly. And yes, she knew the CIA didn't normally get involved in domestic situations—their targets were more internationally focused, and the Special Activities Division had certainly been targeting international groups who were hostile to the US. So much counterterrorism work had been going on with her unit, but...

But I know how the government works. One agency scratches the back of another. She'd wanted to pull in help from other agencies to unravel the mystery of the McGuire murders.

Ronald hadn't helped her. In fact, he'd ordered her to stand down. Only now he was calling up Sullivan? She didn't like that setup. Not at all.

"He gave me the meeting location," Sullivan said. She realized he hadn't answered her question. Probably because he didn't have an answer for her. "The guy is down here, in Austin. Did you know that?"

No, she didn't. "I don't trust him." It hurt to say those words, but they were the truth. "He shouldn't have contacted you."

"He said you wouldn't listen. That he'd tried to warn you, but you kept digging." Sullivan tilted his head as he studied her. "You were digging for me, weren't you?"

Obviously. "You needed closure. It was the only thing you ever seemed to really want—the truth about your parents."

He shook his head. "That's not all I want."

Her gaze slid to Mac, then back to Sullivan. "Why weren't you taking me with you?"

"Because I don't trust the guy, either. I think it's some kind of trap. Maybe a straight setup. And I didn't want you put at risk."

She didn't deny that it could be a trap. With Porter dead and Ronald already on the scene, suspicion was heavy within her.

"Mac will watch my back," Sullivan said. "He'll be there to—"

"Ronald never goes into the field alone. He always has backup, too." Only she was usually that backup. Until she'd started branching out more in the last year.

Making her plan to leave the agency behind. "You need me."

"I need you *safe*."

She shook her head. "I'm not the type to sit on the sidelines. You know that about me."

"Yes."

Resolutely, Celia nodded. "Then it's settled. Mac and I will both be your backup."

He didn't move.

So she just went around him and headed for the back of the vehicle. But before she could reach for the door, he'd raced after her. Sullivan caught her wrist in his hand. "I'm fine with any risk that comes my way," Sullivan said gruffly. "But I am not fine with risking you."

Sweet. But… "I'm not yours to risk, Sully. I'm my own person. I make my own decisions."

"You were hunting to find the truth about my parents—*that's* what put the target on your back, Celia. That's what Ronald said. I did this to you."

"Have you noticed," she murmured, "that you and I play the blame game? I thought it was my fault you were taken, that I should have seen the enemy sooner. And now you… You're trying to put any threat I face on your own shoulders." She shook her head. "We've got to stop that. Let go. Bad things happen in this world." She could hate them. She could rage against them, but they happened. "Maybe we should just focus on *stopping* those bad things now."

He didn't let her go. "I don't want anything bad happening to you."

She stepped closer to him. Her body brushed against his. "Then maybe you should watch my back while I watch yours." Because she wasn't letting him go out to this meeting without her. She knew Ronald. She'd seen him in the field plenty of times.

He could be absolutely deadly.

If the agency did turn on me, it would have been from Ronald's order.

"What if…" His voice lowered as his head dipped toward her. "What if I'm the bad thing that happens to you?"

She didn't understand that, not at all. "Sully?"

"You are too good for me. I've always known that." His fingers caressed the inside of her wrist, moving lightly over her pulse and sending a shiver sliding over her. "Letting you go isn't possible for me. I'll try to be the man you need. I swear, I will."

He was the only man she wanted. Just as he was. "Sully—"

A car horn honked. Loudly. Celia actually jumped, and then her head whipped around. Mac was back in the vehicle and currently blasting away on the horn. He lowered the driver's-side window, leaned across the seat and called out, "Look, I get that the two of you are really into each other—good for you. Fantastic. I was always rooting for you guys. But we have a rather dangerous man waiting for a rendezvous, and I'd really like to see how this damn scene plays out with him." His jaw hardened. "If he knows who killed our parents, the guy *will* be talking to us. One way or another."

It wasn't as if Ronald would just give in to a threat, even a threat that came from the mighty McGuires. But he might talk to her.

Or he might shoot her.

They'd find out, soon enough.

She pulled her wrist from Sullivan's hold. "Time to go."

He swore.

AN ABANDONED WAREHOUSE wasn't exactly a prime meeting spot…unless you were looking for a place to run some shady deal.

No eyes, no ears…no one around for miles.

Sullivan braked the car in front of the warehouse. He'd already dropped Mac off—a good distance back so the guy wouldn't be seen—and he knew his brother would be moving into position. Sullivan hadn't wanted to arrive with Mac in the seat next to him. After all, there was no sense tipping Ronald off to Mac's presence just yet. So he'd taken precautions and made sure to drop off his brother in a secure area.

One that would be hard for Ronald to see from that warehouse.

But Celia had stayed with him. Determined, fierce Celia.

"Are you ready?" she asked him now.

Hell, no, he wasn't ready. He would be *ready* if she was far away, maybe behind half a dozen guards, but Celia wasn't the hiding type. She'd been trained as a fighter, and that was just who she was, straight to her core.

If he tried to push her to the side…no, that couldn't happen. He had to respect what she could do. They'd stand together, and both of them would be stronger for it.

He saw her check the gun he'd given her. Her movements were quick, practiced.

"Ready," Sullivan replied, his voice quiet. There were a dozen other things he'd rather have said to her, but this wasn't the time. It sure wasn't the place.

Later, he'd tell her how he felt. Later, they'd figure this thing out between them.

We can make it work. He'd do anything to make it work between them.

They exited the vehicle and stayed low as they made their way inside the warehouse. The door was unlocked, no doubt courtesy of the welcome wagon that was Ronald. When they pushed on that door, it squeaked open slowly. The interior of the place was dim, dust-filled. Light spilled in from the busted windows on the right and overhead. Sullivan made sure not to step on the broken glass as he made his way forward. He kept his gun in his hand, kept his body alert and waited for the danger to show itself.

"I thought I said to come alone…"

Hello, danger.

Ronald Worth walked through the doorway on the right. He had his hands up, apparently showing that he wasn't armed. Just because the guy wasn't flashing a weapon, it didn't mean he wasn't dangerous.

"I thought you wanted to see me," Celia said, her voice incredibly calm. "So I figured you wouldn't mind if I tagged along."

Ronald Worth was in his early sixties, or at least that was what Sullivan had heard. The guy was damn deceptive in person. He was fit, his hair was still a dark black and his light brown eyes had faint lines near their corners.

Ronald's gaze slid from Sullivan's gun to the one

held easily in Celia's hand. "Are you really pointing that thing at me?"

"Yes," she said flatly. "I really am."

He made a faint rumble of disappointment. "After all we've been through together? Come on now, Celia, I made you into the woman you are."

"No, I did that myself. You were just my boss."

Sullivan kept his weapon aimed at the guy as he stepped forward. "You said you had information on my family."

A faint smile curved Ronald's mouth. "I figured you'd bring her along. I mean, even though I said come alone—that was probably like waving a red flag in front of your face, right? You decided I had to be the threat in this game, so you came running, with Celia at your side." He dropped his hands. "Since that worked so well, it's time to leave."

What?

Ronald's smile tightened. "Come, Celia. I'll have you with a new assignment by dusk. You can slip right back into the fold. No one ever needs to know about this little defection—"

"It's not a defection," Celia fired right back. "I told you after the assignment in North Dakota went sour—I'm done. I've had enough and I want out."

Ronald sighed. "Are you still upset about that presidential hopeful? Look, I was told he was the man to watch. Our job was to get close and look for skeletons in his closet. You found plenty of those. I don't see where the problem was."

"There are skeletons in everyone's closet," Sullivan murmured. "Just like I'm betting there are plenty in yours."

His words drew Ronald's gaze back to him.

"I don't remember saying you should lower your hands," Sullivan snapped at him.

Ronald's gaze hardened a bit. "You're not actually barking orders at me."

"Uh, yeah, I am." He raised his weapon. "Hands *up*."

Ronald lifted his hands. "I have a car out back, Celia. We need to leave."

She took a step closer to her ex-boss. "I'm not leaving Sullivan."

Anger flashed across Ronald's face. "Not that again. Look, so you're still married to him. We can fix that mistake. No problem."

Still married—

Sullivan's gaze cut to Celia.

"The guy is dragging you down," Ronald continued, his voice roughening. "You don't want to be a target like he is. You don't want to get caught in the hell that's coming."

But Celia's expression never wavered. "Why don't you tell me about that hell? Tell us both. You seem to have been holding back on me for quite a while. According to Sullivan, you know who killed his parents."

The guy gave the faintest of nods.

"Who killed them?" Sullivan demanded.

Ronald's eyebrows rose. "It was all in the family."

What in the hell was that supposed to mean?

"Crimes like that, they can be personal. They can be—"

"Stop it," Celia blasted. "You're just jerking us around! His brothers didn't kill them! None of them were even in the country when his parents were murdered!"

"Ava was in the country," Ronald murmured. "Always wondered…just what did she see? So much more than she said, I bet. Only she knew how to keep quiet, not like her mother."

Sullivan lunged forward. He grabbed Ronald and shoved him up against the nearest wall and he put the gun under the man's chin. "Not Ava. I won't believe your lies!"

"Look at him," Ronald said, and he didn't sound even a little scared. Instead, his words vibrated with fury. "Look at what he's doing, Celia! Is this really the man you want to throw your life away for?"

He's pushing my buttons. Playing a game with me.

Celia grabbed Sullivan's shoulder. He let her pull him back.

"Ava didn't kill them," Celia said flatly. "And just so you know, I *won't* pull Sullivan back next time."

Surprise rippled through Sullivan. Celia truly did have his back. *And I'll have hers.*

"Because I think you've been lying to me, Ronald," she added. "You stonewalled my investigation, didn't you? And you worked so hard to get this little face-to-face meeting…was it because you wanted to get close to me?" Her words were calm, eerily so. "Are you trying to kill me?"

"No." The one word seemed torn from her boss. "I'm trying to keep you alive. You stirred up a hornet's nest. You should have left it alone. They all should have. Now I want you out of this mess before it's too late—"

"Who killed them?" Sullivan roared.

Celia stepped in his path. "Sully, let me—"

Ronald grabbed her. He yanked Celia back against him, and in that quick instant, the guy had a knife at her throat.

"Drop your gun, Celia," Ronald ordered her.

She didn't drop it.

Sullivan took aim at the other man. "I will put a bullet in your head." They should be clear on that. "Let her go, *now*."

"I need to walk out of here with Celia," Ronald rasped. "We'll go, and you won't follow."

Sullivan shook his head. "I will follow wherever she goes." Celia still had her gun, and he *knew* she'd be making a move soon.

"I was following orders back then," Ronald said, his words barely more than a whisper. "I didn't pull the trigger. I want you both to know that."

Then he dropped the knife and whirled Celia around to face him. His hands closed tightly around her shoulders.

She pressed her gun to his chest.

"I didn't pull the trigger," he told her, voice desperate. "But it's all coming back on *me*. I wanted you to stop digging into the past. Dammit, as soon as you recruited him, I knew it was a mistake. So I—"

"You were the one who set up Sullivan," she said, her voice hoarse. "You were the one who sold out him and the others agents on that mission. *You* were the one behind it all?"

His jaw locked. "I didn't know you'd married him. Not until later. And when I told you that we couldn't go in after him on a retrieval mission, you should have just listened to me! This could all have been over! You could have been safe! I would have been safe!"

She shook her head. "I think it is over now. For you."

Ronald was there when my parents were killed. "You SOB," Sullivan snarled. "Why?"

"I didn't have a choice," Ronald rasped. "There was too much to lose. And I... He held the power. Back then, and now."

"Don't give me that," Celia said. "You're the director of the Special Activities—"

"And how do you think I got that job?" Disgust tightened his face. "I sold my soul long ago. He got rid of the enemies in my path, and I turned a blind eye when necessary."

The knife had clattered to the dirty floor near them.

"You came here to kill us both, didn't you?" Celia asked. "You're still turning a blind eye, aren't you? Protecting yourself, no matter who else you hurt."

His eyes closed. "I was going to lead you out, and that would be the end for you. Sullivan wasn't going to escape, either."

Lead you out...

"You are dead," Ronald continued, and he actually sounded sad. "You just don't know it. I'm sorry, Celia... really sorry this had to end like this for you..."

Then Sullivan saw a glint from the corner of his eye. He'd been in the battlefield before and seen a glint just like that. *Off a sniper's rifle.*

"Celia!" He roared her name even as he leaped toward her. He grabbed her arm and slammed to the floor with her.

He heard the thud of impact. There was no mistaking the sound a bullet made when it sank into flesh. Once you heard that hard thud, you never forgot it.

Not Celia. Not Celia.

He was on top of her, shielding her body with his own. But Ronald Worth had no shield. And the bullet that *would* have gone into Celia just seconds before had lodged in Ronald's chest.

As Sullivan looked up and watched him, Ronald put a hand to his chest. His legs gave way. The bullet must have gone straight through him, tearing through his organs, because a trail of blood followed him as he slid down that dirty wall, marking a deadly path.

"Celia," Sullivan whispered. She was so still beneath him.

"I'm okay." Her voice was a faint breath of sound. "Get Mac on the line. He needs to know a shooter is out there. We need to warn him."

Celia had told him that Ronald always had backup with him. And that backup was ready to kill.

He eased off her, making sure not to present a target. They were both well away from all the windows now.

That's why Ronald grabbed Celia. To make her a target. Sullivan would bet the SOB had said that if he couldn't get Celia to walk out with him, then he'd pull her into the line of fire.

But I got her out.

"C-Celia…" Ronald rasped her name. "Help me."

Sullivan put his phone to his ear. He knew his brother would have turned his phone to vibrate. Mac wouldn't risk having a ringtone give away his presence. Before the first ring could even finish…

"What the hell is going down in there, Sully?" Mac demanded.

"A sniper is in the area. He just tried to take out Celia, but he hit Worth instead." One glance and he knew… "The guy isn't going to be living much longer. I need you to call your cop buddies and get a team out here. Now."

Before the sniper slipped away.

A ghost who disappeared in the wind.

"Stay alert," Sullivan ordered him.

Celia was creeping toward Ronald.

Sullivan slammed down his phone and grabbed her hand. *"Don't."*

"He's dying," she whispered back to him.

"And he was ready for *you* to die." He pulled her closer to the nearest wall. He needed to get out there and hunt that shooter. "You can't help him, Celia. You know that."

Her hand brushed over his cheek. Sullivan stilled.

"I can," she said. "I will."

"Celia—"

"Go after the shooter. I've got this."

Then she crawled away, heading back toward Ronald. The other man was gasping now as he tried to clumsily put his own hands over the gaping wound in his chest.

The man could still be a threat. He'd been working covert operations for years. Celia had to know just how dangerous the fellow still was. The knife was far too close to Ronald.

Celia kicked the knife away. Then she put her hands over Ronald's. "Look at me."

Sullivan barely heard her voice.

"It's okay, Ronald. You're not alone."

And Sullivan knew just how Celia planned to help the man who'd been ready to kill her.

She wasn't going to let Ronald die alone.

Slowly, Sullivan slipped from the room.

Chapter Eight

His blood soaked her fingers. It was warm, slick, and the flow wouldn't stop.

She'd pulled Ronald down onto the dirty floor. His head was in her lap. Her hands were over his chest.

"Celia…"

"Save your strength. Help will come soon." She'd heard Sullivan tell Mac to call the cops. Any minute they'd be hearing the wail of sirens. "You'll be all right."

His laughter was little more than a rasp. "You know… that isn't…true."

Yes, she did. She also knew that when a man was dying in your arms, you said what you could to comfort him.

Even if he'd just tried to kill you.

"I'm…sorry." Ronald seemed to force out those words.

"Shh…" She didn't want to hear his apologies. She didn't want to open the floodgate on the pain inside her. She needed to be strong now.

"Always…respected you…saw so much…in you…"

She pushed down harder on the wound. So much blood. If Sullivan hadn't grabbed her, she'd be the one bleeding out on that dirty floor. She'd be the one struggling for each breath.

And Ronald would have been the one to send her to her death.

She stared into his eyes. Dark, deep and pain-filled.

She tried to smile for him.

"Celia…" He did smile for her. "You're usually… a better liar…"

And he was usually a better man. "Why?" She wanted to know before it was too late.

"Because you were…destroying me."

She shook her head but never let up the pressure on his wound. "I wasn't. I never did anything to you."

"Past…tied up…a weight that's been pulling me… for so long…"

She stared into his eyes. His breath was coming in slower pants. "How were you connected to Sullivan's mother? Were you—were you the man who killed her boyfriend?"

His bloodstained fingers lifted toward her cheek.

"Talk to me, Ronald." *You don't have time to waste.*

"I'm…sorry."

"Then tell me what you can." She still didn't hear the shriek of sirens. "What was your connection?"

"Her boyfriend…was a target…"

Her breath expelled in a rush. "A government target?"

"Only doing my…job." His eyelashes began to sag closed. "Hired…assassin. We didn't…didn't kill the woman. Let her go… She should never…never have been…there… She…recognized him…knew killer… F-family…"

His eyes had closed. His breath was so hard, so—

There was no sound.

No more hard breaths. No more rasping voice struggling to speak.

She swallowed. "Ronald?"

He didn't answer her. Her left hand slid up his neck and searched for his pulse. Her bloody fingers lingered against his skin, but there was no pulse to feel.

"Goodbye, Ronald," she whispered. She remembered the first time they'd met. His firm handshake when he'd welcomed her into his office. Her knees had been knocking together, but she'd refused to show him her fear. She'd promised him she could handle any job the agency threw her way. She'd been so eager to prove herself.

Carefully, she slipped from beneath him. Celia lowered his head to the floor.

She'd thought she knew him. She'd thought wrong.

Celia wiped her bloody hands on her jeans, then picked up her weapon again. She went after Sullivan.

HE HEARD THE roar of a motorcycle. The distinct sound of the engine couldn't be mistaken, and Sullivan bounded around the corner of the warehouse. A good fifty feet away, he saw the man on the motorcycle— a guy wearing a heavy black leather coat and a dark helmet. There appeared to be a heavy gear bag of sorts strapped to his back.

Not a gear bag. A weapon bag. Sullivan would bet the guy's sniper rifle was in that bag.

"Stop!" Sullivan yelled.

The guy didn't stop. He shot forward on the motorcycle.

Mac leaped from the shadows, his gun up, and fired at the guy on that motorcycle.

The bullets slammed into the bike's body and the rider nearly lost control. But then he revved the engine once more and took off, even as Mac kept firing at him. The guy crouched low on the bike and was vanishing as Mac and Sullivan raced after him.

Hell, no, we won't catch him on foot.

Sullivan spun around. "Go stay with Celia!" he called to Mac. "I'm going after that jerk." Because if that guy got away, they'd be back to square one. No way. No damn way could that happen. He ran back to his car, jumped inside and twisted the key.

The engine sputtered, not starting instantly.

He stiffened.

The car was just tuned up last week. It should have started right away.

His head whipped up. Through the glass of his window, he saw Celia run out of the warehouse. He threw open the door and lunged out of the car. "Back, Celia!" he bellowed at her. "Get back—"

There wasn't enough time for him to get to her. The car exploded behind him, sending a blast of fire rushing right at him. He saw the terror on Celia's face—that one instant seemed to be frozen in time. Her mouth was open, as if she was screaming.

Was she calling his name? He couldn't tell for sure. He couldn't hear her. The blast was too loud, deafening.

But Sullivan could see the terror in her eyes. Her gaze had gone wide, her blue eyes never bigger than they were in that desperate moment.

He'd told her to get back.

She was still rushing forward.

And the fire seemed to surround them both.

HE BRAKED THE motorcycle when he heard the explosion. Through the visor of his helmet, he glanced back and saw the dark cloud of smoke rising into the air.

It had been pathetically easy to predict the moves of the McGuires. Of *course* they would give chase. Of course they'd think they were the unstoppable force who could follow him and save the day.

Like father...like sons.

So while Sullivan had been kept distracted by Ronald, he'd put his little surprise in place. Then he'd waited, giving Sullivan and his brother—because, sure, he'd known Sullivan would have a tagalong with him—a chance to spot him. After all, they couldn't give chase unless they'd actually seen him.

Now the chase was over. For the McGuires, at least.

The smoke kept drifting in the air. In the distance, he heard the wail of sirens. The local authorities, finally coming to the rescue. Only who was left to rescue?

He turned back around. He'd have to go off-road to avoid the cop cars. Easy enough to do. He'd lie low for a bit. Maybe even take refuge at an old cabin he'd enjoyed once before.

And when it was clear, he'd just slip right out of town and get back to the life that waited for him.

But before he left, he'd make sure that the McGuire ranch burned to the ground...a final end to that dark chapter of his life.

No more mistakes.

His fingers curled around the handlebars and he drove away.

"SULLIVAN!"

She heard the cry distantly, a muted call.

"Celia!"

Her eyes opened. She sucked in a deep breath and nearly choked on the smoke. Her breath came out in a coughing spree as Celia realized where she was.

Not on the ground. She'd reached Sullivan. Their bodies were tangled together, as if they'd been tossed by the explosion. They'd landed together, but he was beneath her, and he wasn't moving.

Just as Ronald hadn't moved.

"No." Her voice was so weak. "Sully?"

"*Celia! Sullivan!*" That cry wasn't so muted now. It was Mac's desperate bellow. He was racing toward them.

Sullivan's face was cut. Dark ash and dirt covered his features. Her hands flew over him, frantic, as she searched for wounds. "Sully, please, talk to me."

Her fingers pressed to his throat. When she felt his pulse, her whole body shuddered. He was alive. "He's okay!" Her voice was too weak to carry over to Mac, so she tried again. "Sully is breathing! His pulse is strong." She cleared her throat, pushing back the lump that had risen there as she managed to shout, "He's alive!"

Sullivan's eyes opened. Bleary, but aware.

His car kept burning, sending that smoke billowing up into the air. He'd escaped, just in time. They both had.

"Celia?"

She threw her arms around him and held on as tightly as she could. "You're alive," she said, her voice catching.

His arms rose and locked around her. He held her in a strong grip. Strong, unbreakable Sullivan. Just what would she have done if he'd burned in that car?

The air was heavy with the scent of the blaze. She

could hear the crackle of the flames. She knew the shooter had set that bomb. Ronald wouldn't have had the time to do it.

And Ronald didn't tell me about it. Even as she'd been trying to comfort him in his last moments, he hadn't tried to warn her that death was waiting. Had he known? Had he just not cared?

"You weren't supposed to leave this meeting alive," she whispered. She held him even tighter. "You're a target, Sullivan. Someone is gunning for you." Someone with powerful connections.

Footsteps pounded toward them. "That was too damn close," Mac said, his breath huffing out. "When I heard the explosion, hell, Sully, I thought you were still in the car!"

Sullivan pulled back from Celia, but he didn't let her go. "The ignition sputtered." A muscle flexed in his jaw. "I've heard that same sound before, in the Middle East. The engine sputtered when I was on a mission there…" He coughed, and then rasped, "Back then, I had about five seconds to get the hell out of my jeep before it exploded."

Five seconds.

Five seconds to live.

Five seconds to die.

She shuddered against him and finally, finally heard the sound of sirens.

CELIA DIDN'T NORMALLY spend a whole lot of time in police stations. When she was with the agency, she'd worked her own brand of law enforcement, and it hadn't entailed sitting in a police interrogation room while she was the one being grilled.

But when the cops had rushed to the warehouse and discovered both a burning car and a dead body…she knew that she wouldn't be going anyplace soon. Sure, Sullivan and Mac might have a relationship with the local cops, but she was an unknown.

A potentially deadly threat.

Celia stared at her reflection in the one-way mirror. Her hand lifted as she brushed back her hair. She didn't look completely like hell. Maybe forty percent? Thirty percent like hell? Her fingers rubbed at the soot on her cheek. Her nose scrunched up as she realized she still smelled like fire.

And she still had blood on her jeans.

The door opened and a tall, broad-shouldered African-American man entered the room. He was dressed casually, with a badge clipped to his waist.

"Ms. James…" He pulled out the chair across from her and sat down. He sighed, looked absolutely less than thrilled as he stared at her, then drummed his fingers on the tabletop. "We have a problem."

She had a lot of problems right now, so the guy needed to narrow things down a bit.

"I'm Police Captain Ben Howard," he said, his voice not friendly and not threatening. Just flat. "And I have some questions for you." After that announcement, he just waited.

So she asked, "Um, what are those questions?"

His dark eyes scanned her face. "This is the part where you're supposed to ask for a lawyer."

"I don't want a lawyer." She didn't want to draw anyone else into this mess. "I haven't committed any crimes, so I don't need one."

"You were found at the scene of—hell, I don't even

know what," Ben muttered. "An unidentified male was shot, a bomb was placed in Sullivan McGuire's vehicle and—"

"The dead man isn't unidentified. I knew him quite well." That news probably wasn't going to help her in the suspicion department. "But he was CIA, and if I start talking about him, the talk won't get very far."

He stared back at her. "CIA." Then she was pretty sure he swore under his breath and she caught the mutter of, "Things can never be easy with the McGuires…"

She considered the matter again—as she'd been doing the whole time she was waiting in the interrogation room. "I don't think he was acting under government orders. In fact, I think he was tied to the deaths of Sullivan's parents years ago." Though there was no *thinking* about it. Ronald had confessed. She knew of his involvement with one hundred percent certainty.

Years ago, two men had slipped onto the McGuire ranch and committed those murders. Ronald Worth had been one of those men. And the mysterious shooter? She thought he had been the second man.

The captain stared back at her. "Just how do you fit into this mess?"

"I was CIA, too," she said.

He closed his eyes.

She waited. He didn't open them again.

Her gaze slid to that one-way mirror. Just who was in there, watching them?

"How long will it be," Ben asked, still with his eyes closed, "before federal agents swarm in here and tell me they're taking over my case?"

"I don't think the CIA is aware of what's been happening down here. The the victim you found, he was acting outside his parameters with the agency."

Ben's eyes snapped open. "A rogue agent?"

She swallowed. "So it would seem." Only he hadn't been acting alone. They had to find the shooter.

Before he went after the McGuires.

Her shoulders straightened as she focused on Ben. "You've been talking with Sullivan." She had no doubt about that. "I'm sure he told you what happened." As much as Sullivan could tell him. "I don't see what other information I could provide—" She broke off and folded her hands on the table. "Most of my past is classified."

"Then give me the name of someone at the CIA who can verify what you've told me."

She nodded and rattled off a phone number for him. He wrote it down on a pad beside him. She waited a beat, then said, "Ask for Alexandra Sanchez." Because Agent Sanchez had been a fixture at the agency for as long as Celia could remember. She'd been the supervisor of the Special Activities Division before being promoted up the chain of command. Sanchez would have to be informed of Ronald's death…and his betrayals.

There's going to be a housecleaning at the agency.

"Agent Sanchez can verify my identity for you," Celia said. "But when you call her—"

"Her group is going to swarm and whisk you away, right?"

They'd try.

He rose but didn't leave the little room. Instead, Ben put his hands on the table and leaned toward her. "Are the McGuires in danger?"

She held his gaze. "I believe that they are." Until that shooter was caught, none of the McGuires should sleep too deeply. "A hunter is out there. He's trying to tie up loose ends."

Like Sullivan.

Like me.

"You don't have a name for me? Not a face?"

She shook her head. "I never saw the shooter."

"But you were with the victim when he died, right? Did he have any famous last words?"

She didn't look away from his stare. "Nothing that can help you."

He snatched up the notebook. "I'm going to make that call."

She nodded. When the door shut behind him, she didn't move from that uncomfortable chair. But she did remember…

Only doing my…job. Ronald's last words were replaying through her mind. *We didn't…didn't kill the woman. Let her go… She should never…never have been…there… She…recognized him…knew killer… F-family…*

In the end, it kept coming back to that. *Family.* Just who had made the McGuire family into a target?

"THEY'RE NOT LETTING Celia go," Mac said as he marched out of the police station.

The sun was setting in the city, a red glow that spread across the sky. That glow looked far too much like blood for Sullivan's taste.

"What in the hell do you mean," Sullivan demanded, "they aren't letting her go? They have to! They aren't charging her with anything—"

"They can't even confirm her identity right now." Mac closed in on him and kept his voice low. "Look, my buddy Ben is working the case. He's doing everything possible, but this thing is a nightmare. With Celia's ties to the agency, with Ronald's dead body…hell, you know it's a mess."

"She can't stay in interrogation forever!"

Mac looked away.

Oh, hell, *no*, Sullivan knew he wasn't going to like this.

"They've moved her to a cell," Mac said.

"No." He shook his head. "Celia doesn't belong—"

"Protective custody, okay? That's what Ben is calling it right now. He's trying to figure things out. Seems Celia gave him the name for some lady at the CIA. When he called her, she demanded that he keep Celia secure until she could arrive. And *that's* all he'd tell me. Ben clammed up after that, and I knew he'd already been pushed too far." Mac glanced up at the police station. "We need to go home for the night, man. Check on the family. Try to figure out our next move."

His next move *wasn't* going to be ditching Celia. Ever since they arrived at that police station, he'd been fighting to see her. "I'm not leaving."

"You can't do anything today. The CIA boss they called in should be here tomorrow and—"

"And how do we know that she can be trusted? How do we know that someone won't swoop in here with federal ID and take Celia—then kill her? We can't trust anyone right now. You know that."

Mac focused on him. "We can trust each other. McGuires always stick together."

Yes, they did. And if what Ronald had said was true…if he was still married to Celia… "She's a McGuire, too."

Mac didn't have a comeback for that.

"Would you leave Elizabeth?" Sullivan pressed. "Just walk away while she was locked up and a killer could be closing in on her?"

"There are cops all around Celia. She's—"

"We know cops can go bad." They had personal experience with a cop going rogue. A cop they'd wrongly trusted for years. "Yeah, we have some friends in there, but we both know friendship doesn't always stand up against money or threats. With the right leverage, anyone can turn."

"You can't break the woman out!"

And I can't leave her.

Mac whistled. "Sully, look, you're covered in soot and blood and you smell like a fire. At least just go home and shower. I'll keep watch and make sure she's not transferred out, okay? She won't leave that building, and I know that's what you're afraid of."

Sullivan's back teeth had clenched.

"You're worried the CIA will whisk her away and you won't see her again," Mac added.

"I can't lose her." He knew his voice sounded ragged, but there wasn't much he could do about that tone.

"You won't. I told you, I'll stand watch, I'll—"

But Sullivan had stalked around his brother. He was marching up those steps and heading into the police station.

Mac grabbed his arm and leaned in close. "Sully, don't do anything stupid."

He wouldn't make a promise he couldn't keep. "I'm not leaving until I see her."

Mac searched his face, then gave a grim nod. "Guess it's like that…"

"Yeah, it's like that." And anyone who got in his way would regret it. He stormed back inside the station and cut a path straight to Ben's narrow office. He didn't bother knocking—he just shoved that door wide-open and demanded, "I want to see my wife."

Ben had his phone pressed to his ear. He stared at Sullivan a moment and said, "I understand the full seriousness of the situation. You have my word, the witness will be handled." He swiped a hand over his sweating forehead. "Three, yes, that sounds good."

Sullivan didn't move from that doorway. The last time he'd seen Celia, she was in the back of a patrol car. He'd argued like hell at that scene, but the cops hadn't listened to him. When a dead body was close, they had a tendency to overreact a bit.

"Right. Yes, yes, I understand," Ben said into the phone. "I'll see you then." He hung up the phone and rose. "When a door is shut, Sullivan, it usually means people should stay the hell out."

"My...wife," Sullivan snarled. "You've had her here for hours. She didn't get to speak to an attorney—"

"I brought that up to her. Said most folks asked for one," Ben said as he maneuvered around his desk. "She refused. I *wanted* her to call in a lawyer, but she wouldn't."

A growl built in Sullivan's throat. "You also can't keep her here indefinitely." He was aware of footsteps behind him. Sullivan glanced over his shoulder and saw Mac heading toward him.

"It's for her protection," Ben muttered.

Sullivan's gaze snapped right back to him. "Bull. In your cell, she's a sitting duck for whatever trouble comes her way." He advanced on Ben. "The dead man today? He was CIA. How do you know that the next killer who comes calling won't also be flashing CIA identification? Would you just turn her over to any bozo with a government ID?"

Ben squared his shoulders. "It's not my call to make."

"I want to see her. *Now.*"

Ben raised one eyebrow. "You're giving me orders now?"

Sullivan opened his mouth to reply.

"We all need to calm the hell down," Mac said from behind him.

Since when was Mac the one to give advice on being *calm*?

"We're on the same team here," Mac added. "We all want justice."

Ben nodded. "That's why I wear the badge."

"You put her in a cage," Sullivan said. He hated that thought. Was Celia scared? Was she wondering why he hadn't gotten her out of there? Did she think he'd just walked away?

"I gave her protection. The woman wasn't exactly sharing a lot with me. I got that she was CIA, and then I pretty much got stonewalled because she didn't think I had clearance to learn anything else." Ben huffed out a breath. "I called the number she gave me, all right? *They're* the ones who said to keep an eye on her. Want to know what I was just told about the woman you're claiming is your wife?"

He didn't need to know anything else. He already—

"She's a dangerous threat to security," Ben blasted. "A woman who should be monitored at all times. I walked in there, saw her and thought, *no way is that lady a killer*. But the CIA—the *CIA*—just told me otherwise! And they have someone coming to collect her tomorrow. The sooner she's out of my hands, the better."

Someone is coming to collect her...no, no. "That can't happen. You can't trust them!"

Ben just stared back at him with a troubled gaze. "Then what else am I supposed to do?"

Ben was a good cop, he knew that. The captain had worked with Mac plenty of times and Sullivan had been right there with them. But...

"Are you asking me to go against the CIA?" Ben's voice was soft.

"I'm asking you to let me see my wife." That was all he'd say.

"Come on, Ben," Mac added, voice cajoling. "Five minutes. What will it hurt? If she's locked up, she's certainly no threat to anyone."

Sullivan's whole body was tense. The seconds ticked by and then...

"Five minutes," Ben agreed, "but you McGuires had better not do anything to make me regret this decision."

Chapter Nine

Celia's cell was in the back of the police station, far away from anyone else. There was a toilet to her right. A sink waited close beside it. One saggy cot was pushed near the back wall of the cell.

She wasn't on that cot. Celia was busy pacing. They'd taken her clothes—claiming they were evidence. With all the blood on them, they probably were. Now she was wearing prison gray, and the clothes scratched against her skin with every step she took.

She heard the clang of one of the doors opening and stilled. She'd heard that same clang when they brought her back there earlier. Was a guard returning? Her growling stomach reminded her that she hadn't eaten…

All day.

So maybe someone was bringing her food.

Footsteps came toward her. She strained, listening. Not just one person. Two. Her heartbeat quickened a bit and—

Captain Ben Howard appeared.

She gave him a grim smile. "Got more questions for me?" *And maybe a sandwich?*

"Not this time," Ben said. He stepped aside. "Five minutes."

Sullivan. Sullivan was there.

Celia leaped toward those bars. Her fingers wrapped around them and she held on tight. The smile on her face almost hurt, it was so wide. "Sully!"

His fingers wrapped around hers.

"I'll be back," Ben said. Then his footsteps shuffled away.

She didn't look after him. Her gaze was glued to Sullivan's face. "You still have some ash on you," she whispered. His hair was tousled, his gaze dark and tumultuous, and he'd never looked sexier to her than he did in that moment.

If only they weren't separated by bars.

"You shouldn't be in here," he said, his voice gruff. "I'll get you out—"

"No, you won't, but it's rather sweet of you to say."

"Celia?"

"I'm a woman with no past. I can't even give the cops my Social Security number. And a dead man's blood was all over me." She shook her head. "There's no way I'm going anyplace soon, not until the CIA comes for me."

He stepped closer to the bars. "You know you can't trust them! Why did you tell Ben to contact the agency?"

"Because there are some people there I can trust." She had to believe that, despite what had gone down in that warehouse.

"Ronald and Porter," he gritted out. "Two men from the agency tried to kill you."

"That's why I told Ben to contact Alexandra Sanchez. She was Ronald's boss. If there are others in the CIA—men and women like them who are going to turn and kill—then she has to know about the risk." She leaned toward him. "Alexandra will come and take me into custody. I figure she'll be here by tomorrow morning."

"And I won't see you again."

No, he probably wouldn't. "Not until all this is cleared up." Until the powers that be decided her fate.

"You can't just be taken!"

She didn't want to talk about what might happen to her. "You and your family—you need to dig more into the life of your mother's ex-boyfriend. Ronald said he was the target. His death started this whole chain reaction."

"That twisted joker also said I needed to look to my family for the killer." A muscle jerked in his jaw. "That isn't happening. I trust them all."

She shook her head. "You trust the ones you know, but…what about the ones you don't know? What about the family your mother left behind? Ronald told me that your mother recognized the man who killed Henry Jones. She knew him."

His eyes glinted. "If she knew him, she would have just said the guy's identity—she would have just told the cops who he was."

Maybe. Maybe not. "She went back to see the cops a second time, remember? I told you there was a fire, and all evidence from that meeting was lost. Maybe she *did* tell them the guy's identity…"

"And someone made sure that testimony was destroyed?"

A man like Ronald Worth would've had the power to make the evidence disappear. *Is that why he was angry with me for digging? Was he afraid I'd find some link to that truth? And his involvement?*

"Family." The one word was heavy as it slipped from Celia. "That's what this keeps coming back to, every single time. You have got to find out more about your mother's family."

"There isn't anyone left there," he said. "I already ran the files. She had an older brother, but he was killed in a car accident just before she gave up her life there. Hell, that was probably one of the reasons she was so eager to walk away. There was nothing else left for her there."

She wasn't so certain. "Dig. You'd be surprised at the skeletons you might find."

The captain had said they had five minutes. How much time had passed? "Do me a favor?"

"I'd do anything for you."

In that instant, she believed he meant those words. Her heart ached. "Kiss me."

There was just enough room between those bars. He could kiss her once more.

It would be a kiss goodbye.

Sullivan instantly leaned toward her. His lips brushed against hers, and then that kiss deepened. She hated the bars. If only she could touch him fully. Savor him.

Why had fate been working against them from the very beginning?

She gave herself fully to that kiss, trying to forget everything else in that moment but him. She'd always loved his taste. Loved the way his lips pressed to hers. Her heart galloped in her chest and she pressed ever closer to him. She'd never wanted anyone else more than she wanted her Sully.

The familiar clang reached her ears, and Celia knew the captain was coming back.

She pulled her lips away from Sullivan's. "I'll miss you," she said.

"That *wasn't* goodbye."

Arguing with him would serve no purpose. Her gaze slid over him, memorizing his face. "Keep your guard up, Sully."

He took a step away from the bars. "And keep your trust in *me*, Celia. I won't let you down."

She made herself keep smiling as Ben appeared and led Sullivan away. Her shoulders remained straight, her back upright, and then...

He was gone.

A tear leaked down her cheek.

Sullivan had finally done it. He'd made her cry for him.

No, for what could have been.

"WHAT IN THE hell are you going to do?" Mac demanded as he glared at Sullivan. "Sit on a stakeout at the police station all night?"

Sullivan crossed his arms, leaned back against the brick wall and kept his eyes glued on the station across the street. "They'll take her out the back."

"What are you even talking about?"

"I'll need a ride," Sullivan said, thinking this through. "Preferably a car that won't ignite when I crank it."

Mac coughed. "Yes, right, that goes without saying."

"They'll take her during the night."

"Sully?"

"I know how they work." After all, he'd worked with them before. "Ben was talking to the agency when I went into his office." The guy had been sweating bullets. "He said three. Had to be 3 a.m. That's the time they're coming. And when they get her, I'll be right behind them."

"You're really going up against the CIA? Do you know how crazy that sounds?"

For Celia, he'd go up against anything. "Ronald Worth was there when our parents were murdered."

"Yeah, and now *he's* dead. The family is champing at the bit to talk to you and find out what the hell went down."

"The shooter got away." His eyes narrowed. "Ronald Worth took a bullet to his chest. But before he died, he told Celia that Mom's ex-boyfriend was his target. Target," he repeated. "That's the term you give an assignment." His gut had clenched. "The shooter is tied up with the agency, too—I'd bet my life on it." So much more made sense for him now. "*That's* why I was taken years ago. They kept talking about my family—but it was just because they were trying to see what I knew before they killed me."

"What about the Witness Protection Program?" Mac wanted to know. "They're the ones we need to grill. If Dad was working with them, if that is how he first met Mom—"

"There is no *if* to it." Their father had been so much more than he realized.

"Then maybe their deaths were tied to another case that he worked. Dad's last words were, 'I'll never tell you. No matter what you do. I'll never tell.'" Those words had haunted them all. "Maybe it was someone else's identity he was protecting. Maybe he died trying to keep one of his charges safe." Mac started to pace. "What we need is access to all his old case files."

As if those were just going to be turned over to them. Not without the right leverage, they weren't.

"Go back to the ranch," Sullivan said. "Check in with the others. Pull in every contact we've got. Plenty of people owe us favors. Let's start calling them in."

Mac paused. "And you're going to just stay out here on your own? I mean, could you make yourself any more of a target?"

Yes, he could. "Go back to the ranch," Sullivan said again. "I'm good here."

"No, what you are is obsessed. You need to watch yourself. Celia will—"

"Celia is my priority now." And the second those words were out of his mouth, he realized just how true they were. It wasn't about solving the mystery of his bloody past. For him…Celia was what mattered. Keeping her safe. Making sure she didn't vanish from his life.

Mac gave a low whistle. "Like that?"

"Like that," he agreed.

Mac's stare measured him. "Then how about I get that ride for you…you know…the one that doesn't explode when you turn the ignition?"

SHE ACTUALLY SLEPT. True testimony to just how exhausted she was. But when Celia heard the clang of metal, her eyelids flew open and she jerked up on the cot. It was so dark in that holding area.

Too dark.

There had been a faint light shining when she closed her eyes, but now there was nothing. The whole area was pitch-black.

Footsteps shuffled toward her.

"Don't be afraid…"

That voice—it was the police captain's voice. Ben.

"You're being transferred, ma'am." A bright light shone in her eyes, and she lifted her hand, trying to shield her gaze. "It's for your own protection."

She'd heard two sets of footsteps coming her way. Celia rose slowly from the cot as the cell door was unlocked. "Who's giving the orders for the transfer?"

"I am."

She couldn't make out the second person's form, but she knew that voice.

"You asked for me specifically," Alexandra Sanchez said, "so you got me. You'll come with me tonight, and you'll tell me exactly what happened to Ronald Worth."

Celia had expected to capture the lady's attention.

Now, if only she could be sure that Alexandra wasn't about to lead her off to a slaughter.

As for what had happened to Ronald… "He died." That was what had happened. "Though quite a few interesting twists and turns happened before his death."

"I'm sure they did," Alexandra murmured.

"Do you already have the body?" Celia asked. Because she knew Alexandra would want her own team reviewing Ronald's remains.

"Yes."

The light was still shining in Celia's eyes, and it was annoying the crap out of her. She moved forward and felt someone grab her hands.

"Sorry," Ben said. "But I'm going to need to cuff you for transfer."

Her gut clenched. "Hardly seems like standard procedure."

"None of this is standard," Ben said. "But the order to move you came down from the governor himself…"

"We're old friends," Alexandra revealed. "He was happy to assist me in this matter."

Celia was sure the guy had been only too happy to help the CIA. *Scratch my back…*

"He swore you'd be safe," Ben added. "That's the only reason this transfer is happening."

Right. Because if you couldn't trust the CIA, who could you trust? "I assume you're also retrieving Porter Vance's remains?" Celia asked as the cuffs were snapped around her wrists.

"Yes, when the helpful captain here told me about the body that was recently found near McGuire Securities, I investigated and realized the victim had been… one of ours."

Had been. The emphasis there was a telling one.

"We'll want to compare the injuries that the two men possess." Alexandra's voice was mild. Her footsteps tapped away as they left the holding area. "At this point, it would appear a sniper took them both out. We'll know soon if it was the same weapon, and from the weapon we can find the killer."

That made sense. Many snipers had signature bullets that they enjoyed using to mark their prey.

She was led out of holding and to a back door. It was still so dark. But when that door opened, she saw the alley behind the station.

A black SUV idled near the curb.

"You swear she's not in danger?" Ben asked. His hand was curled around her elbow.

Alexandra Sanchez turned back toward him. Now

that they were outside and the starlight fell down on them, Celia could just make out Alexandra's profile. The woman's hair was pulled back and twisted at the nape of her neck. She wore a long skirt and a loose top. "I give you my word, Captain. I absolutely mean Celia James no harm."

Then Alexandra strode toward the SUV. She opened the back door and waited.

Celia could feel the captain's concern. It was almost touching. "Don't worry about me," she said to him. "I can take care of myself."

"Cuffed?"

She smiled. "You learn a lot as a government agent." Including how to get out of cuffs very, very quickly. "When Sullivan comes back tomorrow—" and she had no doubt that he'd return for her "—tell him it…it still isn't goodbye." Eventually, she'd find a way back to him.

Then Celia turned and headed for the waiting SUV. She climbed into the back. Alexandra followed her and the door swung closed.

"Get us away from this place, Monroe," Alexandra instructed.

The driver waited just a beat then accelerated, taking them away from the station. The silence in the SUV was thick and far too heavy, as it seemed to weigh down on Celia.

Finally…

"I didn't know," Alexandra said quietly. "I assure you, Agent James, I had no idea that Ronald Worth had gone bad. When we had that—that *issue*—years ago, there was never any suspicion that he'd been involved. Now that I know the truth, I've already issued a full investigation into his life. Agents are searching his home even now."

"That issue." Celia nodded as she repeated those words. "You mean when Sullivan McGuire was betrayed and three other agents were killed? When we realized we had a mole in our group?" Not just one mole, though. Another that they hadn't seen. Ronald.

"Yes." Alexandra's voice had hardened. "That issue. If any intelligence had pointed to his involvement, Ronald would have been dealt with immediately."

Celia glanced down at her cuffs. The SUV had just moved beneath a streetlight, and the metal gleamed.

"He was involved in the murder of Sullivan McGuire's parents," Celia said.

A delicate pause. "I'm looking into that."

Celia glanced up. "Look harder."

"Who was the shooter, Celia? Who took out Ronald?"

Her fingers flexed within the cuffs. "I didn't see him."

"But you were with Ronald when he died. Did he tell you who was working with him?"

"No." Her voice was curt. "Where are we going?"

"A safe house. I'm not transferring you out of the area just yet…"

Her shoulders brushed back against the seat. "Because you're too busy doing housecleaning at the agency?"

"Every case Ronald ever worked will have to be reviewed. Every member of his team—past and present units—will need to undergo a thorough investigation. If he sent Porter down here on an execution mission for you, then that means he could have been using other agents to do his dirty work, too. Everyone who has been working with Ronald is under suspicion."

Celia understood exactly what was happening. "A nightmare."

"And it's just beginning." Alexandra exhaled heavily. "I don't know how deep this goes. I don't know who in that unit is loyal to the organization or who was just a puppet on a string for Ronald. Every single person must be vetted."

"Where do I come in?" Celia asked. Part of her was afraid to find out.

"You're dangerous," Alexandra said flatly.

Some days. True.

"You're obviously a threat. Ronald thought you knew something that would incriminate either him or the shooter he'd been working with. And that fact means you're valuable. Valuable *alive*."

"So I am in protective custody," Celia murmured. Her gaze slid toward the front of the SUV. The driver appeared to be completely focused on the road, but she knew he would be closely monitoring their conversation.

"He's been vetted," Alexandra said. "And because of his personal connection to the McGuires, I thought Monroe could be of assistance to me. This tangled web is closing around them, after all."

Monroe. The name clicked for Celia. She'd recruited Monroe Blake herself. An ex-SEAL, the guy had been a perfect candidate for the Special Activities Division. Tough, fearless and with a drive that had impressed everyone in the unit, Monroe had fit right in with the team.

Monroe braked the SUV at a red light. "I know Davis," he said, his rumbling voice carrying back to them. "He's a good man, and when Alexandra briefed me on what was happening, I volunteered to haul butt down here to help."

It was great that he said that, but Celia was past the point of taking anyone at their word.

"It hurts, doesn't it?" Alexandra asked her. "When you look around and realize that everyone else could be as good a liar as you are."

She'd been trained to lie by the agency. "Covers were a natural part of this business. Turning on your teammate wasn't."

The light changed and Monroe accelerated.

"The shooter needs to be brought in alive," Alexandra said. "I'll personally handle his interrogation. He'll tell me just how deep this thing goes."

"It's not like he's just going to offer himself up for capture," Celia pointed out. If Alexandra thought so, she was living in a dream world.

"No, he won't." Alexandra paused a beat. "That's where you'll come in. Let's just see how eager he really is for you to be eliminated from the picture."

Ah, now it made sense. Celia fully understood just why she'd been whisked out of that jail cell by the most powerful woman in the CIA.

It wasn't about being kept safe.

It was about being used as bait.

SULLIVAN WAITED UNTIL all the lights were off in the little house at the end of Juniper Drive. He kept his vehicle well hidden, and he stayed in the shadows of the old trees that lined the street. There'd been a flurry of activity in that little house before, but all was silent now.

Celia was in that house. He'd seen her go in.

She hadn't come out.

He checked his weapon. It sure was getting ever harder to tell the good guys from the bad in this little game. He wasn't going to take any chances. He would be getting Celia out of there. Until she was back at his side, he felt as if he couldn't draw a deep enough breath. Fear gnawed at him. He knew both of them were in the sights of a killer.

Together, they'd be the stronger team.

He slipped toward the house. He'd studied the exterior for a while, looking for the best spot to gain entrance, and right now…he went to the side window. A quick swipe of his knife and he'd cut the screen. Would the house be wired with an alarm?

If so, then when he lifted that window, everyone inside would know he was there, but…

But he hadn't seen any signs of an alarm. The house had been taken at short notice, so he wasn't thinking that full precautions had been implemented, not yet.

Sucking in a deep breath, he reached for the lock on that window. Breaking it wasn't hard, and then he just pushed that window right on up…

No alarm shrieked and his breath slid past his lips.

SHE HEARD THE creak of the old wooden floor. Celia hadn't been asleep in that little bed; her mind had been too busy spinning. But when she heard that creak, her eyes strained to see in the darkness and she reached under the mattress, searching for the knife she'd insisted on getting before Alexandra left her.

I won't stay unarmed.

Alexandra had slipped her the knife before she

walked away. She'd also gotten rid of the cuffs, a very good thing.

There were no more creaks. Only a heavy silence, but Celia was sure someone was closing in on her. Moving closer and—

A hand pressed to her mouth. Rough, hard, strong.

She swung up with her knife.

"Baby, try not to cut anything vital."

That rough whisper belonged to Sullivan. She stilled instantly, the knife probably far too close to his throat.

"Good, I appreciate that restraint," he muttered.

She dropped the knife and threw her arms around him. Celia yanked Sullivan down on the bed with her as her heart galloped in her chest.

"Knew you were in here, smelled the sweet flowers as soon as I opened the window," he rasped, his breath blowing lightly over her ear.

She smelled like flowers? No way, she probably smelled like a jail cell. She was even still wearing her prison gray! Alexandra had promised to bring her new clothes come morning, but—

The lights flashed on.

She blinked, trying to adjust to the sudden brightness.

"Get the hell away from her," a hard male voice snarled.

Sullivan tensed against her. "I'm guessing there was an alarm set to go off when I opened that window, after all." But he didn't sound particularly concerned. Very slowly, he eased away from her. "Must've been a silent alarm."

"Drop your weapon." That was Monroe barking the

orders, because he was the guard who'd been left to make sure she stayed alive.

And didn't escape. Not until Alexandra came up with a full plan, anyway. *A plan to use me.*

"The thing is," Sullivan drawled, "I'd rather not be unarmed."

Monroe glared at him. "Look, fellow, this isn't a debate, it's—"

A man came up behind Monroe, moving fast, a dark shadow that rushed into the room. Monroe sensed the threat too late and whirled.

But a heavy fist drove into his jaw and Monroe fell back, slamming into the floor. Before he could lurch to his feet, Sullivan had his gun aimed at the guy's head.

"Sullivan, stop!" Celia leaped toward them. "You don't need another enemy!"

Monroe wiped away the blood that dripped from his mouth. "I recognize that hook…" His gaze slid toward the man who'd sneaked up behind him. "It's been a long time, Davis."

Her gaze swung between them.

Davis gave Monroe a grim smile.

"You know this joker, Davis?" Sullivan demanded. He didn't lower his gun. And he still looked enraged.

"His name's Monroe," Davis offered. "And he saved my hide a time or two."

"And you saved mine." Monroe slanted a glance Sullivan's way. "Sure didn't expect you to find her so fast."

"I never lost her." Finally, his weapon lowered. "And you need to do a better job of checking for tails. I'm not the only one who could have followed you back to this place."

Monroe flushed. "I did check for tails. You're just… good." That admission was grudging.

"Right. I'm good. So good that I'm about to walk right out that door with Celia." Sullivan caught her hand in his and threaded their fingers. "Come on, baby, let's go."

He stepped forward.

And Monroe moved into their path. "Sorry." He rubbed his jaw. "But that can't happen."

"The hell it can't. You aren't keeping Celia here! You don't get to hold her against her will!" Sullivan blasted. "You don't—"

"He's not," Celia said quietly, cutting through his words.

Sullivan's head whipped toward her. "What?"

"I'm not here against my will. I'm here because I wanted to be."

The poor guy still looked confused.

"Monroe is an agent with the Special Activities Division. He's working for a woman named Alexandra Sanchez. For all intents and purposes, she *is* SAD now." She pushed back her hair. "She's the one who got me out of the police station, and she's the one tracking the shooter."

Davis swore.

Right. So Davis had obviously figured out where this was going, and, based on the darkening of Sullivan's face, he knew, too.

"The shooter wants me dead," Celia said. "So I'm going to be the bait to draw him out."

It was odd. She'd never seen Sullivan's eyes go quite that glacial before. Fury was supposed to be hot and burning, but his—his gaze was ice cold.

"Out," Sullivan growled.

Her eyebrows rose.

"Davis…take your buddy Monroe and get out," Sullivan ordered, his voice far too quiet. "My wife and I need to have a little chat."

She flinched. *Wife.* That one word got beneath her skin.

"Uh, wife?" Davis seemed to focus on that word, too. "I mean, I know it's been a busy twenty-four hours and all, but did I miss something? Celia said you were divorced—"

"She's my wife." His hand tightened on hers. "She's *mine*, and I want to talk to her, alone, right now."

"You aren't going to change my mind," Celia said.

He didn't reply.

But Monroe and Davis headed for the door. She glared at them. Just because Sullivan said jump, it didn't mean everyone had to leap so high. He was just a man. An angry, coldly enraged man.

The door closed behind Davis and Monroe. Jeez, so much for Monroe being her protection. *Way to abandon me in the face of danger!*

But they were gone, and she was suddenly alone with a very different Sullivan. She'd never seen him quite this way before, and for an instant, she hesitated.

Chapter Ten

"No," Sullivan said instantly. "That can't happen. It can't."

"I—"

He pulled her closer to him. "You can't be afraid of me." But he was seeing the fear in her eyes as she gazed up at him. "Anything but that. I will *never* hurt you."

Her breath whispered out.

She was wearing a gray prison uniform. Her hair was pushed away from her face and her eyes—those big blue wonderful eyes—drifted slowly over his face.

"How well do we know each other?" Celia asked him.

"No one knows me better," he said flatly. "Not my brothers. Not my sister. You know me, inside and out. I haven't hidden my dark spots from you. You're the only one who has ever seen me just as I am." And that was why he couldn't bear her fear. He needed Celia to accept all of him.

Just as he would accept all of her.

"Then you should know," she said, "that I have to do this."

"There's no need for you to be put at risk!"

Her smile was bittersweet, those dimples almost

painful to see. "We don't have this man's face. Not his name. He's got a cover firmly in place, one he has hidden behind for years. But he's come after me. He thinks I know something—he must believe I uncovered something that can expose him when I was digging for you." She gave a little shrug. "As long as he believes that, then we have an advantage. He has to keep coming for me, and when he does, we can be ready for him."

"Celia—"

"He's a ghost now. One that has haunted you and your family for far too long. I'm going to stop him."

He absorbed that. "I don't want to change you."

Her lips parted.

"Because I happen to think you're pretty damn perfect just as you are."

The fear was gone from her eyes. He couldn't decipher the emotion that had replaced it.

"I'm not about forcing you to hide, because you're right, that's not you." He brought her hand to his mouth and pressed a kiss to her knuckles. "But I will be at your side. You're not being the bait when it's my family at the center of this mess. He wants me dead, too. That bomb was in my car. You and me, Celia. Together. We'll go after him together or not at all."

Her gaze fell to her hand, cradled so close to his lips. "I always feel...warmth when you touch me."

He felt a whole lot more than just warmth when he touched her.

"Sometimes I wouldn't even realize I was cold, and then you'd be there." Her lashes lifted. "I like it when you're near. I like it when you touch me."

His brother was right outside that door. The other

guy—Monroe—was no doubt trying to eavesdrop and figure out what move Sullivan would be making next.

And the move he wanted to make? Getting Celia into the bed that waited just a few feet away.

Not here.

"We're leaving," he said as he cleared his throat. "Your new guard can come with us. Davis backs him up, and if you think he's on our side…" He let those words trail away.

"I don't have any reason to doubt him. Or Alexandra."

That wasn't exactly a ringing endorsement, but Davis had seemed sure of the fellow.

"The guard can come with us. Only him, no one else." Because he wasn't ready to put his trust in Alexandra. "The ranch is a hell of a lot safer than this place. I'll take you there, and then we're not going to be bait." He gave her a grim smile. "We're going to be the hunters."

Alexandra Sanchez rode the elevator up to her suite. It had truly been one hell of a day. This scandal was going to nearly destroy the Special Activities Division. Ronald Worth had certainly made a mess of things.

The elevator dinged and the doors opened. She'd used a special card to access this floor, and she clutched that key card now as she headed into the hallway. The lush carpeting swallowed her footsteps.

At least Celia James was settled for the night. Monroe would keep a close watch on her. He was a good man, and one of the newer recruits. More important, he was a man she knew personally. She'd been involved in

Monroe's life for years. She could vouch for him, and she knew that Monroe would not let her down.

The hallway was dead silent. At this hour of the night, most folks were already asleep. She wanted to crash herself, but there was too much work to do before she could fall into bed.

Too much.

Retirement was starting to look pretty good to her.

Alexandra opened the door to her suite. She hurried inside.

She'd taken five steps before she realized she wasn't alone.

He'd been as still as a statue, so she hadn't even noticed him. Or maybe—maybe it had just been far too long since she was actually in the field. She'd lost her killer instinct.

Before she could flee back into the hallway, he managed to grab her. His arm locked around her neck and he yanked her up against his body, holding her tightly.

"You are so easy to predict," he said, his voice rough and his breath blowing against her ear. "Ronald told me that you always believed in doing things first-class. Once I realized you'd been called in, it took me no time to figure out which hotel you'd be in." He laughed. "And a little bribe to the desk clerk got me your suite number."

He was cutting off her air supply. She kicked back, but he moved, easily avoiding her defensive maneuver. She tried to slam back with her elbow, but he just laughed again.

"Oh, now, come on, you can do better than that. Or have you gotten soft...sitting behind that big fancy desk for all those years?"

She wasn't soft. She twisted hard and managed to break free of him.

But he kept her purse. And her weapon.

In a flash, he had that weapon pointed right at her.

He smiled. "You don't usually remember the ones who do the dirty work, do you? I spent a lifetime doing that dirty work…so much time. That blood will never come off my hands."

"You haven't worked for me," Alexandra said definitely. Though there was something very familiar about him. Her gaze swept over him and lingered on his eyes.

Her heart beat even faster.

He just shrugged. "These days, I'm really more of a free agent."

She inched back. She could grab the nearby lamp and use it as a weapon.

"I know you talked to Celia. I know you *took* Celia from the police station. Because, see, when I slipped in to finish her off, she was gone." He sounded angry. Maybe she could use that anger against him. "Just what did she say to you?"

He thinks Celia knows who he is. She'd let him keep believing that. "Celia stayed with Ronald until he died." She gave him her own grim smile. "You know how it is when death is so near. People always want to unburden their souls." He wasn't supposed to be here. She wasn't the bait. Celia was. Only…

He couldn't find Celia, so he came after me.

She should have stayed at that little safe house with Celia and Monroe.

"He confessed?" the man demanded.

Alexandra hesitated. He'd come here without a mask.

He'd stepped right into the light to show his face to her. She knew what that meant.

He doesn't intend to let me leave this room alive.

But she wasn't going down without a fight.

"What do you think Ronald did?" Her chin jutted into the air. She'd spent her life fighting to make the world a better place, and yes, sometimes she'd gotten her hands dirty and sometimes she'd done things that didn't make her proud.

But she'd never been a coward and she'd never, ever backed down from a fight.

You think I'm easy prey? Think again.

"I think he didn't have a long time to live, not after my bullet ripped into his chest."

"He lived long enough," she allowed.

She hated his smile. Alexandra inched a bit closer to the nightstand. *He is familiar. Too familiar.* Those eyes…even his smile… For an instant, grief burned through her.

"You're going to tell me where Celia is."

"You're going to give yourself up," she said in the next instant. "Because you have no idea what kind of enemy I am. You have no—"

He shot her. The bullet tore out of the gun—her own weapon—and slammed right into her chest.

She looked down, truly shocked for an instant. The blood was already pumping from her wound. Alexandra grabbed for the bedcovers as she slid to the floor.

He stalked closer to her. He grabbed her hair and yanked her head back. Then he put the gun right between her eyes.

"I don't care who you are," he said. "I don't care what kind of power you *think* you have."

He'd missed her heart. It was still beating. Painfully, so very fast. But beating. "I…know…" Alexandra tried to say. *I know who you are.* Too late, she understood.

"That's right, you know. And you *will* tell me where she is. Celia and Sullivan McGuire won't destroy me. I'll destroy everything and everyone around them before that happens."

"Before we leave, I have to check in with Alexandra," Monroe said. "There's no way I'm letting Celia walk out of this place without official approval."

Celia slanted a quick glance toward Sullivan.

"By the book," Davis muttered. "Still play that way, huh, Monroe?"

"There's nothing wrong with that!" Monroe snapped. He had his phone pressed to his ear. "I happen to respect my boss, and until she gives the all clear—" He broke off, frowning. "The call went to voice mail."

A shiver slid over Celia's skin.

Monroe dialed again. "Look, I know where she's staying. I'll just call Alexandra's room directly." But his words held an edge now, and Celia could feel his worry.

Alexandra wouldn't ignore his calls. Not with everything going on.

Davis stepped toward him. "Where is she?"

"The Wattley Hotel. She told me that she always stays there when she's in town."

Celia's breath caught. "And Ronald would know that! He might have told the shooter…" It made sense. He could have told the shooter all about the habits of those in power at the agency.

Learn everyone's weaknesses.

And if the guy knew Alexandra Sanchez was in town...

"She's not answering," Monroe said. The edge in his voice had gotten worse.

Maybe she can't answer.

Celia and Sullivan were already running for the door. "Call the desk clerk!" Celia yelled. "Make him get someone up to her room!"

Because she was worried the shooter had already gone after another target.

"YOU JUST MISSED a call, Alexandra," he said as he picked up her phone and stared at the screen. "Monroe Blake. I'm guessing that's one of your agents, hmm? Is he the one guarding Celia?"

Every breath was a struggle. Her hands pressed to her chest. He hadn't hit her heart, but she was bleeding so much.

Is this the way Ronald felt, at the end?

"Alexandra! Look at me!" he snarled.

Her gaze jerked to him.

"Is Monroe the agent guarding Celia?"

She glared at him. She wasn't going to give up Monroe or Celia to this killer.

"He is, isn't he?" He smirked at her. "We're going to call Monroe back. You're going to tell him that there has been a change of plans. He has to bring Celia to you."

"No." She had to keep Monroe away from the killer. Monroe—he was her responsibility. She'd promised his mother that she'd always look after him. *I can't let this man get Monroe. I can't fail Susan that way!*

"Yes. You're going to do it, or else I will make you suffer every single moment until I finally put a bullet in your head and put you out of your misery."

"Won't…call…" She wouldn't do it. No matter what, she'd protect Monroe. And where was the help? He'd just shot her—surely someone had heard the noise! There had been no silencer on the gun, but…

Maybe no one else is on the floor. I paid for privacy. Unfortunately, she'd gotten it.

"I'm dialing," he murmured. And he had pushed the button to return Monroe's call.

She prepared to scream. To give Monroe a warning—

But someone pounded on her door.

Someone did hear the shot!

"What the hell?" the man next to her muttered. And he ended the call. He kept the phone in his grip as he headed for the door.

His attention wasn't on her now. So she crawled back, moving toward the lamp.

"Mrs. Smith?" a voice called out as a knock sounded at her door again.

Mrs. Smith. What an obvious alias, but she'd always enjoyed using it. So simple. Why waste time with an elaborate cover when a simple name change did the trick?

She tried to clear her throat so she could call out, but only a whisper escaped from her lips.

The man who'd shot her was right at that door. In another moment, he'd be yanking it open. The hotel employee out there—the poor fellow—would find himself facing off against a killer and probably dying.

She threw her body against the lamp. It wove and crashed down, shattering.

"Mrs. Smith!" The cry of her pretend name was nearly frantic now. "We're coming in! And I've got a crew with me, we're—"

The shooter opened fire, blasting right through the door.

"GOVERNMENT AGENT!" MONROE BARKED when they got to the Wattley Hotel and found chaos waiting for them on Alexandra's floor. "Get the hell *back*!"

And the crowd did. They were on the top floor, they'd just left the elevator…and Celia could already see the blood.

There were some uniformed cops on the scene, but they looked shaky. One cop—a young woman with dark hair—had her hands pressed to the bloody shoulder of a fellow who appeared to be the desk clerk. Or maybe the concierge. He was wearing a well pressed hotel uniform and a name tag. *Justin.*

"What happened here?" Monroe demanded. "Where's—"

A gurney burst out of the suite up ahead. Celia's breath caught when she saw the form on that gurney. Alexandra Sanchez had never looked more vulnerable. Her face was chalk white, her body shuddering. And the blood—

Alexandra's eyes darted around the scene as her gurney was pushed toward the elevator, and her frantic stare locked on Celia and Monroe. "Not…here…" she gasped. "He's…watching…get away!"

Sullivan's hands closed around Celia's shoulders.

"The guy just came out of that room, shooting!" Justin's voice rose. "He was crazy. Just—just firing and then running straight for the elevator!"

If the shooter had been in the elevator, then maybe he'd been picked up on video surveillance. Maybe they could get the guy!

Monroe hurried to Alexandra's side. "I'll stay with you. It's going to be—"

"Get…her…out…" Alexandra ordered, her voice far too weak. "He could still…be here… Get…away…both of you…away! Leave…me."

The EMTs pushed her into the elevator and they all hurried to follow. Their group closed in around Alexandra and the EMTs as the elevator rushed down to the ground floor. "Tell us…who was he? What did the guy look like?"

Monroe's face had turned to stone as he stared at Alexandra.

Alexandra's stare drifted between Sullivan and Monroe.

"Please, Alexandra, stay with us." Celia could feel the other woman slipping away. She caught her hand and squeezed. "You saw him. Describe the shooter. What did he look like?" Celia held tight to Alexandra. "Please, tell us." Alexandra was the key and—

"H-him…" Alexandra whispered. Then her eyes closed.

THE AMBULANCE ROARED away with a scream of its sirens. Celia stood in the shadows of the hotel building, her arms crossed over her chest and her gaze on that ambulance.

Sullivan approached her slowly. "Celia?"

"There's so much blood and death. Sometimes I feel like it's all I know."

More wounded—Justin and a security guard—were loaded into the back of the second ambulance.

"One day," she said, voice soft, "it would be nice not to worry about a killer. Not to think about attacks or danger."

The second ambulance pulled away.

"But that day won't be today," she added.

He put his hands on her shoulders and pulled her back against him. "The hotel staff members are going to be all right." He'd checked out their wounds. Superficial. The shooter hadn't been trying to kill them.

He'd just wanted them out of his way.

But Alexandra…she was a different matter. They'd have to see just how much of a fighter she could truly be.

"Is your brother checking the security footage?" Celia asked.

"Yes." And Alexandra's last whispered word kept replaying in his head. What had she meant, the shooter looked like him?

"I've been looking at every face. Checking out every person I see. He knows me, but I don't know him. Hardly seems fair."

No, it didn't seem fair. Nothing about this mess did.

The hotel doors slid open and Davis hurried out. One look at his grim expression and Sullivan knew he hadn't recovered any usable footage.

"The guy is good," Davis said.

Monroe was right behind him.

"He disabled the security feed before he went up to

the suite. There's no sign of him on the videos. Nothing at all we can use."

Monroe expelled a frustrated breath. "And the hotel staff couldn't identify him. When he started shooting, they ducked. They never even got a look at his face."

"You need to follow the ambulance," Celia said. "She's defenseless now—"

"I've already got a call in to the CIA," Monroe said. "A whole team will be swarming soon."

"But she doesn't trust a team," Celia insisted. "She trusts you. She's still alive, and we need to make sure she stays that way."

His hands were clenched at his sides. "She gave me an order. I'm supposed to stay with you."

Sullivan's shoulder brushed against hers. He needed to be close to her. Her words were haunting him. *There's so much blood and death. Sometimes I feel like it's all I know.* "I'm with Celia," he said flatly. "You need to follow that ambulance and take care of Alexandra. Right now she's the only one who can identify the killer. As soon as she's stable, she can give us the guy's full description and we can find him." His lips thinned. "We just have to make sure that she does wake up. We can't risk him going after her again."

"That's why she needs you," Celia insisted to Monroe.

Davis had his phone out. "And that's why I'm calling in Mac. I want him at that hospital, too. The more people we have that we can trust on scene, the better."

Monroe's eyes glittered. "You're asking me to go against orders."

"Sometimes you have to," Celia said, "in order to do what's right."

Like when she'd gone against Ronald to save him. She hadn't known the guy was a twisted jerk at the time...

She'd just been doing right by me.

Monroe gave a ragged sigh. "You're going back to the McGuire ranch?"

Celia's gaze cut to Sullivan.

"Yes," he said. "She'll be with me." They both needed to crash and regroup before they started their hunt. "I'll guard her, you can count on it. I'll always have her back."

Just as she would have his. He knew that with utter certainty.

IT HAD WORKED, just as he'd planned. By attacking Alexandra, he'd managed to draw Celia right out into the open again.

He stared at their little group. Did they truly think they were safe in the shadows? He'd spotted them the minute they pulled up. The CIA was ridiculously predictable with their black SUVs. Whether abroad or at home, those vehicles truly screamed *look at me*.

The group was separating. Again, something else he'd anticipated. Alexandra—tough agent that she was—had still been clinging to life when she was loaded into that ambulance. Someone would follow her to the hospital. They'd probably stalk around and try to keep her safe.

There was no point in keeping the dead safe. She wouldn't survive until dawn. Her wounds were too grave. She wouldn't be talking about him to anyone else.

So he could move on to his main target.

The McGuires...he figured they'd be going back to the ranch now. Just what he wanted.

So fitting. They thought they were safe out there. So well protected behind their security measures. They couldn't be more wrong. He knew that ranch too well.

After all, he'd been there before. Many times. He'd even killed there.

The ranch is my hunting ground.

They wouldn't see him coming.

But plenty of people would see the flames he left behind.

THE HOSPITAL WAS a scene of total chaos. Monroe Blake had burst through the ER doors just moments before, following the gurney that held Alexandra Sanchez.

At the CIA, Alexandra had always been revered. Respected. And feared. No one had ever gotten close to her there. But—

I share a past with her. As long as he could remember, Alexandra had been in his life. She and his mother had been friends. Always close through the years. And when his mother died, it had been Alexandra who took him in. She'd encouraged him to become a SEAL. She'd brought him into the CIA and the Special Activities Division.

To the rest of the world, he acted as just another agent when he was near her. But...

Alexandra is my family.

And he was afraid she was slipping away from him.

Desperate, he reached out and grabbed her hand. Why had he never noticed just how fragile Alexandra was? She'd always seemed larger than life.

Until now.

"Sir, you need to step back," one of the doctors said. "We have to get her in the OR now."

He didn't want to step back. "Alex..."

Her lashes lifted. Her dark eyes met his. Still alive. Still fighting.

"You should...go..." she whispered. "Told you..."

And he'd ignored orders, for the first time in his life. "You need me."

Tears gleamed in her gaze. He'd never seen her cry before.

"S-sorry..." Alexandra said. The docs and nurses were pushing her gurney toward the OR, and Monroe was running right with them. "Should have... protected..."

Why in the world would she be apologizing to him?

"He's...always...been looking..." Each breath she took was a painful rasp. "Always...searching...never thought he'd...find..."

"Who, Alexandra? Who did he find? Celia? Sullivan?"

"Y-you..."

A doctor grabbed his arm and pulled Monroe back.

Alexandra's gaze lingered on his. He could see her fight to keep her eyes open. "Go...stay with...Mc-Guires...*family*..."

She was giving him another order. Protect the Mc-Guire family. "I want to stay with you."

She gave a sharp shake of her head. *"Family!"*

She was his family. She was—

The OR doors burst open as the doctors took her inside.

THEY'D JUST PULLED onto the ranch's property when Sullivan's phone rang. He lifted it to his ear even as he kept one hand wrapped tightly around the wheel. "Sullivan."

"She's in surgery." Monroe's voice was ragged. "As soon as I know anything, I'll call you."

"Stay with her—"

"Alexandra kept saying for me to come to you! That's her order...*and I'm here because I can't leave her*."

There was such pain in the agent's voice. *This is personal.*

"She's all the family I've got," Monroe muttered.

Family. It could come in all shapes and sizes, and Sullivan knew the bonds weren't just about blood. "Mac is coming to the hospital. He'll help you, in any way you need."

"What I need..." Now Monroe's voice hardened. "What we all need is for this SOB to be stopped. He can't get away from us. He doesn't get to kill and walk."

"No," Sullivan agreed. "He doesn't."

He ended the call and drove the vehicle forward. He didn't head for the main house, though. Instead, he drove them toward the guesthouse.

Her pain-filled sigh almost hurt to hear. "I'm the one who got her down here. I'm the one who thought she'd be able to help me—help *us*. Alexandra kept SAD going for so long. With Ronald dead, I knew she'd come back to investigate and keep everyone on track. Now..."

Now if she died, the whole unit would fall apart.

He couldn't help wondering...had that been the shooter's goal? Just how much was really at play in this deadly game?

"I respect her," Celia said. "And she deserves so much more than that pain-filled death."

The headlights cut through the darkness and fell on the guesthouse. He braked and killed the engine, but neither one of them made a move to leave the vehicle.

"I keep thinking about what she said," Celia whispered. "When we asked her to describe the man, she said—"

"She said he looked like me," Sullivan continued. Those words had stunned him.

"Maybe Ronald wasn't lying."

His eyes narrowed in the darkness as he strained to make out her expression.

"He said we needed to look to the family. We haven't done that, Sullivan."

"My brothers—"

"I'm not talking about Grant or Davis. Not Mac, not Brodie. Not you."

He waited.

"You didn't know that your father worked Witness Protection. Maybe there's more you don't know about him, too. Maybe…do you think it's possible you could have family members out there that you don't know about?"

His heart felt as if it were encased in ice. "You're saying my father might have another son."

"I'm saying Alexandra stared right at you—she used the last bit of her strength to tell you the killer's description. And Ronald—what did he have to lose? At the end, he said it was family. All this time, I think you've been searching too far away for the killer. I'm wondering if, all along, he's been closer than you realized."

As close as blood.

He shoved open his door and headed around to her side of the vehicle. Before he could open that door, Celia was already rising. His hand brushed against her back. They were safe at the ranch. As safe as it was possible to be, and there, he could let down his guard.

"I needed to be close to you," Sullivan confessed.

Her hands rose and pressed to his chest.

"When I thought that you were going to be taken from me…" His jaw ached because he'd clenched it so hard. "Nothing else mattered to me. Finding you. Getting you back—that was it."

"Let's go inside," Celia said.

Right. Inside.

But…

She took a few steps away from him, heading toward the guesthouse.

He stared after her. The stars were glittering overhead. There was no smoke from a car bomb. No scent of blood and death.

It was just them.

"Do you think we're still married?" Sullivan asked, his voice gruff.

She paused and gave a faint, sad laugh. "It's kind of funny…but to tell you the truth, I always felt like we still were."

She had to be careful what she said. Did the woman realize how close she was pushing him to the edge?

Over that edge?

"Even when we were apart, I still felt connected to you. No matter what I did, no matter how many times I told myself to let go, you were still there." She turned toward him. "Why couldn't I let go?"

He stalked toward her. Sullivan lifted his hand and brushed back the hair that blew over her cheek. Before, they'd been all about passion and need.

But desire alone—it didn't survive that long. It didn't last for years.

"I want you to make love to me," Celia said.

Love. For him, that was exactly what it was. The reason he hadn't ever been able to let her go. He'd been far too caught up in Celia from the beginning.

His Celia.

"Always," he said, and Sullivan leaned down. His lips brushed over hers. He didn't push. Didn't consume. He just savored her. If he could have frozen one moment in time, it would be the moment when he kissed her. When he tasted her lips and a surge of warmth filled him.

His eyes were closed and her soft body pressed to his.

"Come inside," Celia said.

As if he needed another invitation.

He followed her in and stopped to secure the guesthouse. He put his shoulders back against the door and stared at her as she stood in a pool of light. There were so many things he wanted to know about her. The past hadn't gotten in their way before. He'd been too focused on the moment, the present with her.

But now he wanted more.

He wanted to secure a future with her.

"I—I need to shower first," Celia said. Then she touched the prison garb she still wore. "And this has got to go."

She turned on her heel and headed down the hallway. A few seconds later, he heard the roar of water in the shower.

He started to follow, already yanking up his shirt.

The floor creaked a bit beneath his feet. By the time he reached the bathroom, Sullivan was already naked.

So was Celia. Naked and under the spray of the shower. Her back was to him, so he had a perfect view of her graceful back and her truly inspiring hips and rear. Such perfect curves.

Steam drifted lazily in the air.

Celia glanced over her shoulder at him, and she smiled.

There was something about that smile. It froze him a moment, then made his heart beat in a double-time rhythm.

"Come closer," she urged him. Nothing had ever tempted him more.

As soon as he saw the doctor, Monroe knew she was gone.

The doctor's face was grim as he approached. Monroe stood. Mac and Davis McGuire were at his sides.

"The damage was too extensive," the doctor told him quietly. "I'm sorry, but she's gone…"

Davis put his hand on Monroe's shoulder, squeezing tightly.

And Monroe lost the last member of his family.

You bastard. I will find you. I will make you pay.

Chapter Eleven

The water pounded down on her, washing away the terror of the day. She forgot about fire and death and being caged behind bars.

She looked into Sullivan's eyes and she couldn't look away. She didn't want to look away.

The water was warm on her skin. The steam had filled the air around her.

And she wanted him.

Celia turned fully toward Sullivan, exposing her body to him. She felt no shyness. With him, she never had. She wanted him to see all of her.

Still married?

In her heart, they always had been. She'd never been able to give him up. She'd always been willing to take any risk, for him.

Her gaze dipped down and she saw that he was more than turned on for her. Good.

Her smile stretched.

Sullivan could always take her away—to a world of only pleasure. A world that consisted of only them.

She needed to be taken right then. Taken so far away.

He stepped into the shower with her. The water poured over them both and her hand lifted, sliding over his skin. He bent to kiss her, a hot, openmouthed kiss that only fanned the flames of her desire for him.

Her hands slid over his body. She wanted to touch every bit of him. His scars still hurt her—she hated to think of him suffering—and she bent to kiss them as the water slid over her back. She stroked his aroused flesh. Celia loved his strength and that raw power, but when he gave a deep, rumbling growl in his throat...

She just stroked him all the more.

"Celia."

She'd always enjoyed playing games with him. Seeing how far he could be pushed. How far he could push her.

Sullivan caught her hands. He pushed her back against the cold tile wall of the shower. She gasped at the contact, and then he kissed her. Deep. Hard. The way she liked.

He freed her wrists and his hands curled around her hips. He lifted her up, holding her right there, and his mouth still took hers even as he positioned his body at her core.

He drove into her. Her legs wrapped around him.

Pleasure.

Desire.

More.

He withdrew, then thrust into her. The water made their bodies so slick. Her breasts pressed to his chest. Her nipples ached for him. Her whole body ached.

Thrust.

Withdraw.

Her hands weren't against the tile any longer. She was holding tightly to his shoulders, and her nails were sinking into his skin.

Every movement of his hips sent him sliding right over the center of her need. Her climax was rising, building and building...

He kissed a heated path down her neck, and she lost it.

Celia screamed when her climax hit.

And Sullivan...let go. She felt his control splinter as he thrust hard, deep, again and again, and it was fabulous.

No fear.

No regrets.

Only pleasure.

His body stiffened. He drove into her once more and she saw the pleasure wash across his face. For an instant, his green eyes seemed to go blind with that surge of release.

Their breaths heaved out. The water kept spraying down on them.

Her legs slid—rather limply—away from his hips. She felt like falling into a little puddle right there. Her body was sated and her mind had finally stopped spinning.

She blinked the water out of her eyes—surely just water from the shower and nothing more—and stared up into Sullivan's gaze.

I love you.

She wanted to say those words so badly.

But then he kissed her. Such a sweet, tender kiss.

A few moments later, he turned off the water. Very carefully, he dried her with a towel, then yanked that same towel roughly over his body. When she stepped out of the shower, he lifted her into his arms.

She didn't need him to carry her. She'd never needed

anyone to do that. But she liked being in his arms, so she relaxed her body against his. Her arms curled around his neck.

Soon they were in the bedroom. He lowered her onto the mattress. Turned off the lights. Then they slid under the covers together.

Exhaustion pulled at her. She just wanted to close her eyes and drift away, but at the same time, she wanted to stay exactly where she was. Awake and aware with Sullivan. She felt as if a clock were on, the time running away too quickly. She needed to reach out to him—

So she did. Celia put her head on Sullivan's chest, right over his heart so she could feel and hear that steady beat. His arm wrapped around her back and he held her there.

Warm and safe.

"There's so much I want to know about you…"

She smiled at the rumble of his voice. "Ask me anything." Her answer was soft. Sleep pulled at her.

"Where were you born, Celia?"

"A town called Jackson, Mississippi." She hadn't been back there, not in so long. Would it still be the same if she returned? Would she still smell the magnolias drifting in the wind?

"What happened to your family?"

Pain tried to pull at her, but she pushed it away. "My father died in an accident at work. At the sawmill." She wouldn't think of that horror—a horror that had scarred a child. "I was seven. My mother never got over it." She'd turned to a bottle to escape the pain. Booze. Pain pills. Whatever she could get her hands on. "She…she was in a car crash when I was thirteen."

A one-car accident on a lonely stretch of road.

Strangely enough, when Celia had gone back years later to read that accident report, she'd learned there was no alcohol or drugs found in her mother's system that night.

But she'd gone off the road and driven straight into that telephone pole. Not stopping, not even trying to brake...

"What was foster care like?"

She thought of that for a moment. Her eyes drifted closed. "Lonely." She didn't even think of filtering her words. With him, why should she? "I was never part of a family. Not really. Always just the girl looking through the glass at the others." Wondering what it would be like to belong.

To be loved.

Was it any wonder she'd been such perfect pickings for Ronald? With no one to notice when she disappeared, she'd slipped right away into a life that...

Was full of secrets.

Lies.

"It was hard for me to make friends. To really connect with anyone." Why? Maybe because she'd been afraid.

Afraid they won't like me, not really. Not when they see who I truly am.

Afraid I'd lose them. Afraid if I cared, it would hurt more.

She'd stopped being afraid with him.

His steady heartbeat reassured her.

"You connected with me."

Even as her breath evened out, Celia smiled. "Yes."

"Why?"

"Because you've always been different." His heartbeat drummed beneath her. And very slowly, Celia slipped into sleep.

SULLIVAN KEPT STROKING her hair. He felt the exact moment when Celia gave in to sleep. "You've always been different, too."

Special.

He stared up at that dark ceiling and he tried to figure out just what he'd need to do in order to keep Celia in his arms forever.

Just as his eyes began to close, his phone rang, vibrating lightly on the nearby nightstand. His hand reached out and he grabbed it, answering it before Celia could wake. "Sullivan…"

There was a pause and then, "She didn't make it," Davis said softly.

Hell. Another victim. Another loss.

Another sin the killer *would* atone for, one way or another.

AFTER HE ENDED the call, Davis walked through the hospital. People brushed by him, nurses and doctors intent on their patients. They hardly gave him a second glance.

That was just one of the things he didn't like about these places. They were so busy. It was incredibly easy for someone to slip in and get close to a vulnerable patient.

He rounded the corner and saw Monroe Blake sitting in one of the waiting room chairs. Monroe's shoulders were slumped and he'd put his fists against his eyes, seemingly propping up his sagging head. The guy was taking Alexandra's death hard, so very hard, and Davis wished there was something he could do for him.

Monroe was a good man. Davis could still remember the smell of blood and death that had been around them on their missions. Monroe had never hesitated. He'd never backed away from any mission.

He'd also never looked beaten.

Until now.

Davis paced toward him.

Monroe stiffened and glanced up at him. His golden eyes swept over Davis, then slid away. "I've been informed," he said, his lips twisting, "by the new authority at the Special Activities Division that I'm supposed to be standing down on this case. With Alexandra gone, my involvement is over."

Davis sat next to the guy. "I figured that call would be coming in, sooner or later." He'd hoped for a bit later.

"Because I knew where she was, right?" Monroe sighed. "That puts me on their suspect list. Some pencil pusher back in the office—a guy who has never seen fieldwork—figures that I just turned on Alexandra and let her die."

"You didn't."

"No," Monroe said grimly, "I didn't. I respected the hell out of that woman. I would *never* hurt her." He held Davis's stare. "Ronald Worth would have known her habits. *He's* the one who told the killer where she was."

Yes, Davis rather suspected that had been the case.

"They're sending in a team. This mess is a huge embarrassment for SAD. They want me on a plane back home, and they said they have *people* who'll be taking over the investigation."

People Davis wouldn't trust. He didn't know them. "What are you going to do?"

"I don't have much choice!" Monroe fired back. "I

was given orders. Stand down." His lips twisted. "And stay the hell away from the McGuires. Apparently, your family is seen as some kind of major threat right now."

Davis made a noncommittal sound. "What do you think will happen to Celia?" That was a question that had to be answered. He already knew Sullivan wasn't just going to let Celia be taken into government custody. Hadn't they all learned that lesson already?

"They want her back." Monroe's voice was gruff. "Everyone sure as hell seems to think that Celia can identify this guy, but I heard her talking with Alexandra. Celia was adamant that she didn't know his identity."

Davis watched a nurse bustle by in the hallway. She appeared frantic to get to her patient. "Sometimes," he said slowly, "you have to make a choice." He rose.

"Davis?"

"You have to decide which orders you are going to follow…and which ones you're just going to forget."

Monroe shook his head. "You act like I have some kind of choice here. I'm not a free agent. I'm a government employee. Do you know what they'll do to me if I go off on my own?"

Davis shrugged. "Oh, yeah, I have a pretty good idea. I mean, Celia went off on her own, didn't she? Then all of a sudden she had folks gunning for her. Strange, isn't it? That the folks in authority up there aren't scrambling to solve this case? Instead, they're too busy covering their own backs. They want this case erased, not closed. It's an embarrassment. You know what went down, so I'm suspecting that when you get back to that fancy office—you know, the one that hides all the bloodshed—they'll probably ship you off on an immediate new assignment. You'll go overseas, and you won't come back until everything about this case is nothing more than a memory."

Monroe rose. "Alexandra deserved better than that." Emotion cracked in his voice and grief darkened his eyes.

"Because she was your mentor, right? The woman who pulled you into the group?"

"She knew my mother," Monroe said as his chin notched up. "Alexandra was always looking out for me. My whole life, she was there for me."

Davis hadn't realized the connection was so personal. "Then I am especially sorry," he said quietly, "for the loss you're suffering." He gave a slow nod. "And if you should decide you want to fight for justice for her…then maybe you should come and join a family that understands that battle."

He turned and took a step away.

"You're telling me…what? To throw away my job with the Special Activities Division? To turn my back on them?"

Davis glanced over his shoulder. "Actually, I'm saying let's give this thing twenty-four hours. We've got a killer out there, one who is champing at the bit. The plan that Alexandra had—to draw him out into the open— it's not bad. It can work. We just need the right team in place."

Monroe's hand rubbed over his jaw. "And this team?"

"You want to join it?"

Monroe's gold eyes gleamed. He seemed to consider that offer for a very long time. Davis just waited.

Then Monroe nodded.

"Then welcome to the family," Davis murmured.

Monroe swallowed. "Alexandra…before she died, she told me to protect your family. To stay with the McGuires." He nodded. "And I will. I swear, I will."

"CELIA…"

Her eyes opened. The faintest streaks of light drifted through the window.

"Not…her…"

She pushed up in the bed. She was pretty much sprawled on top of Sullivan, and she winced, ready to apologize, when she realized—

His eyes were still closed. He was talking in his sleep again. Saying her name.

She eased a bit away from him as her gaze swept over him.

"Let me go!" Sullivan suddenly yelled out.

Celia jerked back.

"Have to get…Celia!"

"Sully?" she whispered as she reached out to him. "It's okay, I'm right—"

"Have to make…her pay…"

There was such fury in his words.

Pain knifed through her, but her fingers gently stroked his shoulder. *I've paid more than you know.* For crimes that hadn't even been her own. "It's okay," she said again, keeping her voice soft.

"Celia…"

Her hand stilled. There hadn't been fury in that one word. There had been longing.

Her eyes stung.

"Love," he whispered. His hands had fisted around the covers. "Love…Celia…"

She almost fell out of the bed. One moment he was

raging against her, and the next—declaring his love? Not possible, of course. Sullivan was just trapped in some twisted nightmare. She needed to wake him up. He didn't love her.

Did he?

Her hand curled around his shoulder and she lightly shook him.

He jerked beneath her touch and grabbed for her. In a flash, he had rolled her beneath him and pinned her hands on either side of her head.

And this is why you don't wake up a person in the middle of a nightmare...especially if that person is a tough ex-marine...

"Hi, there," Celia whispered softly. "Remember me?" She offered him a gentle smile when he blinked blearily down at her. "I'll take that as a yes."

"Celia." He immediately released her and sat up in bed. "Baby, I'm sorry, I was—"

"Dreaming."

"Reliving hell."

She sat up, too, grabbing for the sheet to cover her chest. "That hell you were reliving...you called my name."

He climbed from the bed. He turned on the light and dressed, his movements jerky as he yanked on a pair of jeans. Then he stilled, pausing near the side of the bed as his gaze lingered on her. "I usually call your name in my sleep."

Because you still blame me? Or because you love me? She licked her lips. "Want to talk about what happens?"

"I'm back in that pit. They're slicing me open and I can't get away."

Yes, definitely the stuff of nightmares. "I'm sorry."

"They're telling me that you're involved. That you sold me out."

She didn't move.

"And then…" He expelled a rough breath. "Then it changes and gets all twisted. Because they're saying they are going to hurt *you*. That they're going to kill you, and I know I can't let that happen."

"They…threatened me?" He'd never told her that before.

Sullivan shook his head. "That just happens in my dreams. My worst nightmares." He edged even closer to the bed, and his hand curled under her jaw. "Because that *is* my worst fear, you see. Something happening to you."

"Why?" She needed him to say the words. While he was awake. Fully aware. Staring into her eyes. After everything that had happened between them, she had to hear those precious words.

"Because I love you. More than anything else. And I can't lose you."

She leaped from the bed. Celia wrapped her arms around him and held on as tightly as she could. "I love you," she whispered.

His hands locked around her. The grip almost too tight. "Celia?"

"I love you. I never stopped loving you." Though she'd tried. But the emotion had lingered within her and when they'd been pushed back together, it had flared to life again, stronger, deeper than ever before. "Why do you think I took so many risks? Why do you think I worked so hard to unearth the truth about your past?"

She eased back a bit and stared up at his face. She'd never seen that expression in Sullivan's eyes before.

Hope. So much hope. Enough to break her heart.

"I wanted to give you the one thing you wanted most…because I loved you so much."

But Sullivan shook his head. "*You're* the thing that matters most. It's you, I just realized the truth too late."

"It's not too late." Not for them. Not for what could be. "It's not."

"You're too damn good for me," he gritted out. "I made so many mistakes…"

"We can start again. We *have* started again." She smiled up at him and laughed. "We can do anything."

His gaze swept slowly over her face. "I missed that sound. So much."

Her laughter faded away.

"Your laugh is the most beautiful sound I've ever heard. Just the memory of it got me through too many dark nights."

"You don't need a memory any longer," she said, her heart feeling as if it were about to burst right out of her chest. "You have me. We can make everything work. Together, we can do this. We'll stop the killer. We'll put the past to rest and we'll have the future that we want."

Together…

His head lowered and she leaned eagerly forward, wanting to feel the crush of his lips against hers. Their lips nearly touched. She could nearly taste him.

And someone was pounding on the door. Knocking so hard. Totally and completely ruining the moment.

"My brothers," Sullivan growled. "They must have seen me turn on the light. I swear, they all have the worst damn timing."

She laughed again, unable to help herself. She just felt happy, even if they had been interrupted. *He loves me.* "It's okay. I'm not going anywhere, Sullivan. We have nothing but time." She eased away from him. "Go answer the door. I'll get dressed." The smile just wouldn't stay off her lips. *He loves me. He loves me!*

But Sullivan didn't move. "I want the danger over. I want to find the shooter and make sure he's locked away so that he can't hurt anyone again." His fingers slid down her cheek. "You're in this mess because of me."

No, she was involved because of the choices she'd made.

"There's something else you should know…" His voice had deepened. "A call came through while you slept. I'm sorry, baby, but Alexandra didn't make it."

For an instant, she couldn't breathe. Pain knifed through her, so sharp and deep.

"We *will* get the bastard."

Celia gave a grim nod. *He has to pay. For all the lives he's destroyed. He must pay!*

The pounding grew more insistent.

"Dammit…" His fingers fell away. "Let me go find out what the hell is going on out there…"

She watched him walk away. Sullivan. *Her* Sullivan.

At the bedroom door, he paused and looked back. "I meant what I said before, Celia. Only I should have given you those words long ago. I love you."

Then he headed out.

For an instant, she just stood there. Then she wiped away the tear that had fallen down her cheek. *Alexandra.* The grief wanted to pound through her, consume her, but she couldn't let it. Not now.

She squared her shoulders. Took a deep breath. Pushed past the pain.

I'm so sorry, Alexandra.

Her eyes kept burning as she hurried toward the closet. When would the death stop? The fear? How much longer would it go on?

Celia dressed quickly, pulling a pair of old jeans and a shirt from the closet. Then she shoved up the skirt on the bed. She'd seen another pair of tennis shoes under the bed the other day. Those shoes had to be more comfortable than the ones she'd been given at the police station. She snagged the shoes from under the bed, put them on and then—

Something else was under the bed.

Frowning, she eased down a bit more as her eyes narrowed. She could see the glowing digits of a clock beneath the bed.

That clock hadn't been there before.

Why would a clock be under the bed? The question pierced through the grief she felt.

And her heart stopped. No, that wasn't a clock. Goose bumps immediately rose on her arms.

The digits on that device were counting down so quickly. A small box, with wires coming out the top and those numbers flashing on the top...

A bomb. Dear God. It's a bomb. Hidden under the bed, where no one should have seen it, not until it was too late.

Terror exploded within her.

SULLIVAN YANKED OPEN the guesthouse door. "Seriously, *stop* that damn pounding!"

Davis didn't look particularly concerned about his

snarl. His brother just raised his eyebrows. "So sorry, bro. Didn't mean to disturb your beauty sleep with the little matter of a life-and-death situation. My bad."

Behind him, Monroe Blake grunted.

Sullivan leaned against the door frame. "Give me ten minutes, and then Celia and I will meet you up at the—"

"Run!"

His head snapped back at Celia's shout. He glanced over his shoulder.

"Get out!" she said as she rushed toward him.

"What the hell?" Davis demanded.

"There's a bomb under the bed!"

No, that wasn't possible. They had the best security imaginable—

She grabbed his arm and yanked Sullivan out of the door.

Monroe and Davis were already running up ahead.

"It had five minutes left on the timer," Celia panted out. "Five minutes!"

If his brother hadn't come pounding on the door, they'd still be in the guesthouse. In the bedroom. They'd be—dead?

They ran toward the bluff, but halfway there, Sullivan stopped.

Celia was still holding his arm, so she staggered to a stop, too.

"Sullivan!" Her eyes were so wide. "You didn't see that thing—it is going to destroy that guesthouse! We have to get away."

But his mind was whirling. "Someone got on our property." He didn't doubt Celia's words, not for an instant. He was never going to doubt her again. "If he got to the guesthouse, he could've gotten to the main house, too." His gaze flew toward the main house.

"Brodie's in there," Davis yelled. "Jennifer and Jamie—*they're inside!*"

Horror washed through Sullivan and he tore off after his brother, rushing as fast as he could for the main house. Maybe there wasn't just one bomb. Maybe the killer had placed more around the ranch.

Five minutes. That wasn't long enough. He had to get his family to safety.

Five minutes. Five damn minutes.

Celia was racing to keep up with him. Davis and Monroe were both hurtling toward the main ranch house.

Home. Family. Life. He'd been tied to this place for so long. It couldn't go up in flames like this. He couldn't let it happen.

How did he get in? How did he get past all our security?

Davis didn't stop at the door to the ranch house. He kicked the thing in and roared, *"Jamie! Jamie!"* There was terror in his voice as he bellowed his wife's name.

Sullivan bounded into the house after him.

"What's wrong?" Brodie demanded as he rushed out of the hallway. Jennifer was at his side, her hand clutching her robe. "What's happening?"

"Get out of the house!" Sullivan yelled at them.

Davis had run in search of his wife.

"There's a bomb in the guesthouse," Celia shouted. "There could be one here, too. We have to go!"

And Davis was running back. He had Jamie in his arms, holding her tight. She looked stunned and scared and—

"Is anyone else in the house?" Monroe demanded.

They were all rushing for the door.

"No one else," Brodie yelled as he pushed Jennifer in front of him. "Just us."

How much time had passed? How much damn time?

They were outside now. Running fast and frantically toward the bluff. Part of Sullivan was waiting for the heat of the blast to wash over him. And another part of him…he feared that bullets would rip out and hit him. This would be the perfect time to attack. While they ran. While there was no cover and—

Boom.

The blast shook the earth all around them and flames rushed into the sky.

And those flames were blazing when the first shot was fired.

Chapter Twelve

"Get down!" Sullivan bellowed. It was just as he'd feared. The guy who'd set that bomb was close by, waiting to pick off any survivors.

Now they were all out in the open, with no weapons, sitting ducks for the killer who waited in the woods.

Brodie grabbed Jennifer and yanked her behind the branches of the sprawling tree.

Davis curled his body around Jamie, and they hit the ground, staying as low as they could for cover.

Monroe was right beside Sullivan, and they were both hurrying to reach Celia. That first shot had lodged in a tree just inches away from her head. The second shot could come at any moment.

Celia spun toward Sullivan. Her eyes were wild, frantic, and she lunged toward him, her arms outstretched as if she could reach him.

He saw the bullet hit her. Time seemed to slow down as the blood soaked her shirt. The boom of the gunfire was distant. Everything was distant.

Celia was calling his name.

He grabbed for her, held her tight. "Baby, no!" He fell to the ground, covering her with his body because there was nowhere else to go. Staying low was their best chance of survival.

She trembled beneath him.

His heart shattered.

But then—

Gunfire. Blasting. Not gunfire that had been aimed at them, but...

His head turned. Monroe had drawn his gun and was firing into the trees—right at the spot where the shooter must have been hiding. The direction and the angle were right based on Celia's wound.

That bastard shot her!

And now Davis had joined Monroe in the gun battle. Hell, yes, both men were armed and firing—giving the others cover so they could run for better protection.

"Stables!" Brodie snarled.

Right. It seemed as though there would be less of a chance that the stables would be wired to blow, but, hell, Sullivan didn't know for certain. He just had to get Celia out of the line of fire.

He scooped her up into his arms. Davis and Monroe blasted out their shots, moving with Sullivan and shielding the group as best they could.

"Hold on, Celia," Sullivan urged her. "Baby, you're going to be okay."

Then they were rushing into the stables. The smell of fresh hay permeated the air, and the horses neighed nervously.

Davis yanked the big doors closed behind him.

And Sullivan gently lowered Celia to the ground.

"I'm okay," she said. She even tried to smile up at him. "It's just a flesh wound."

They'd promised not to lie to each other again. But

he stared into her beautiful eyes and said, "Just a flesh wound. Nothing to slow you down."

Then, carefully, he pulled back her shirt.

His breath expelled in a rush as he examined her. And relief nearly made him dizzy. It *was* a flesh wound. One that was bleeding far too much, but nothing vital had been hit.

"Mark will see the flames," Brodie said. He and Jennifer were close by. "His men will notice the smoke, and they'll come running."

Yes, Sullivan knew that was true. Mark Montgomery was their closest neighbor. And Ava—she'd be with her husband when he rushed over to investigate the flames.

Would the shooter be waiting for them, too?

"Call them," Sullivan ordered curtly. "They can't come here blindly!" He didn't want his sister walking into an ambush.

Davis already had his phone out.

"I'm okay," Celia said to him once more.

His hand sank into her hair and he leaned close to her. He kissed her then—deep, hard and fast. "If you hadn't been, I would have gone insane." A simple fact. He needed her to function. When he'd seen the blood, fear and fury nearly maddened him—

I need Celia.

Behind him, he heard Monroe talking into his phone, too. The cavalry would be coming—local cops, government officials. Hell, maybe all of them. But the shooter was always two steps ahead...

"He's going to vanish again," Celia said quietly. Her face had paled, but her eyes burned with her usual fierce passion. "If we don't stop him, he'll vanish...and come back again."

He knew she was right.

Celia locked her jaw and started to rise.

Sullivan pushed her right back down. "Hell, no, baby. *Hell, no*."

"But I can—"

"You can fight the world, I know it. But this time, for me…*don't*." Because she was already wounded. And she was *his* world. He couldn't stand any additional risks to her. "Stay here. I know this land. I can find him."

"How the hell did he even get on our property?" Brodie wanted to know. "We installed the security system—there is no way he could just have snuck past our safeguards without setting off an alarm."

It would seem the guy was just as familiar with the land as they were.

And once more, he thought of what Ronald had said… "Family," he whispered.

"What in the hell does that mean?" Monroe snapped, his eyes gleaming. "Look, I get that you all are tight, but there is one very skilled killer out there. He's taken out trained agents, and now he has us pinned down. For all we know, these stables could be set to blow any minute. Maybe we didn't escape into them…maybe he deliberately corralled us in here. Maybe he's just waiting. No timer this time, but a bomb *he* sets to explode."

The bastard could be planning anything.

Sullivan's gaze slid back to Celia. Gently, he brushed back her hair. He had to keep her safe. He had to protect Celia and the rest of his family.

"We need dogs," Celia said. Her breath seemed to come faster, harder. "Bomb-sniffing dogs to search the entire ranch."

Yes, the whole place would have to be checked. There could be more deadly surprises just waiting for them. Maybe that was what the SOB wanted.

To see them all burn.

Then he plans to shoot any survivors. He wants to take us all out.

"What in the hell did we miss?" Sullivan demanded. Who was this killer? A man who'd been after their family for so long. A man who seemed determined to destroy the McGuires.

He could still hear the crackle of flames coming from the guesthouse.

The hunter out there wanted to see them burn. Maybe Monroe was right. Maybe the jerk had corralled them all into the stables. *The better to kill us off?*

Too bad. None of them would be dying.

He knew he had a choice to make. He could go out there and hunt the shooter. Track him down. He could leave Celia inside with his brothers while he searched.

I don't want to leave her. She needs me.

He needed her.

Yeah, he could hunt or…

I can work with my family. Together, the way we've always done things. No one would be left behind. They'd all be safe. His gaze jerked around the stables. The horses were neighing louder, shifting in their stalls.

"Get the saddles," he ordered. "Because we're getting the hell out of here." Moving targets were so much harder to hit.

And we won't just wait for an attack.

THEY'D ESCAPED THE BOMB. Celia had gotten them out of that guesthouse. Then the whole damn group of them had come racing across the ranch. He'd fired, desperately, because he'd needed to stop Celia.

But he hadn't.

I missed again.

He'd wanted her heart. He hadn't gotten it. She'd survived. The woman was so much harder to kill than he'd anticipated.

Now they were in those stables. Hunkering down. No doubt planning their next move. He hadn't put a bomb in the main house—he hadn't been able to get close enough before. There hadn't been any time.

So I went for Celia. I knew she thought she was safe in that little guesthouse.

She was wrong.

I've been too soft. I should have attacked them all sooner.

They'd be calling in backup. The rest of the family would swarm. They'd close ranks. It would just keep going and going...

Unless no one was left.

He pulled out the detonator from his pack.

No, he hadn't been able to get to that main house.

But he had been able to plant explosives in the stables. Just in case. He'd always believed in having a contingency plan in place.

He stared at those closed doors of the stables. For a moment, the past swam before him. He and Ronald had hidden in those stables. They'd waited until they thought it was a good time to make contact. He'd gone in. The rage had taken over.

I fired before I even thought about it. My finger squeezed the trigger, and she was just gone.

There was one thing that he'd regretted—and that had been her death.

Stop it. Focus. It's you or them. You or them!

He pressed the button to detonate, and when the stables exploded...

He could have sworn he heard his sister scream. But then, he'd been hearing her scream in his dreams for years. Some sins really did stay with you.

No matter how hard you tried to bury the past.

SULLIVAN HELD TIGHT to Celia, keeping a firm grip around her body as the horses bolted away from the blaze. They'd barely cleared the back of the stables when the place erupted, raining fire and chunks of debris down around them. The horses were going nearly wild now, so desperate to escape from that heat.

He didn't head back toward the front of the ranch, or to the main house. Instead, Sullivan and the others surged into the line of trees. That would be their cover. Their protection.

The horses' hooves pounded over the earth. He risked a glance back over his shoulder, and he saw the flames shooting into the sky.

Just another few moments, and they would have been dead. Celia. His brothers. Jennifer. Jamie...

All dead.

It has to stop.

Fury twisted within him. No one attacked his family like this. No one came to their home and tried to destroy them.

His horse surged forward even faster. He controlled the animal easily even as he pulled Celia closer to him.

He directed the horse to the right. He was going

to the main road, but by a different path than the one Davis and Brodie would take with their wives. Sullivan had wanted the family to separate—that way they wouldn't present an easy target in case the shooter found them again.

They would be safe and—

Someone raced out of the brush. A man who appeared to be little more than a shadow. He lifted his gun and fired.

But Sullivan had already leaped from the horse. He'd taken Celia with him and he rolled, twisting his body so she was protected and he hit the ground first. The impact knocked the breath from his body.

A shot rang out. One, two—

He looked up and saw Monroe take a hit in the stomach. Monroe's gun fell from his hand and he rolled off his horse. The horse galloped into the darkness, rushing away.

Monroe groaned and began to rise from the ground.

And the man aimed his gun right at Monroe's head. "This wasn't even your fight."

"Stop!" Celia cried. She'd leaped off Sullivan and, even with her wound, she was rushing toward the shooter. "Just…*stop*!"

He immediately swung the gun toward her.

And Sullivan's world seemed to end.

DAVIS HEARD THE thunder of the gunfire, rising even above the flames. He drew back on his horse's reins.

Brodie stopped beside him.

Jennifer and Jamie were close, edging their mares toward them.

Davis's head turned. "Northeast," he said. His blood had iced. Two shots had been fired.

He was supposed to keep going to the main road. To safety.

But no way was he leaving his brother now. He turned his horse. Everyone did, as if on cue. And they took off, riding fast, so fast.

IS THIS WHAT it was like for my father? In those last moments, when a masked shooter aimed at my mother? When she was taken from him?

Sullivan rose slowly. "Don't."

The flames were still raging in the distance. The horses were long gone. And the gun was too close.

But the shooter hasn't fired. Not yet.

Sullivan put his hands up and walked forward. "It's my family, right? We're the ones you've always been after. *Family.* The McGuires. I'm the one you want to kill." He stepped in front of Celia.

"No, Sully," she said, her voice desperate.

"Me," he said, "not her." He made sure his body fully blocked hers. This guy would not hurt Celia again, not without going through him first.

Monroe groaned and tried to push himself to a sitting position.

The shooter still hadn't fired.

Where are Davis and Brodie? Did they hear the shots? Or had the flames been too loud?

"Just like your father," the shooter snarled. "Always trying to play the hero."

"My father was a good man," Sullivan said simply. "And I'm not playing anything." He had his hands up.

"You want to shoot someone? Fine, do it. Shoot me, but not her. She never did anything to you. *Not her.*"

"She set this nightmare into motion again! She should never have gone digging—"

"She did it for me." Because Celia loved him, and he—he would do anything for her. *Even take a bullet.*

Sullivan stared at the man before him. The guy had a mask over his face. The two men who'd come for his mother and father that long-ago night—they'd worn masks, too. Ava had seen those masks. "You killed my parents," he said.

Laughter. "And I'll be killing you, just like I did them."

"Sully, no." Celia's hands pulled against him. "Stop it! Not for me. *Not for me!*"

Didn't she get it? Everything that he did, it was for her. He'd protect her with his last breath. He'd give anything and everything for her.

"Two lovers," the guy snarled. "You thought you'd get to be happy, didn't you? Just like *her.*"

And Sullivan knew the shooter was talking about his mother.

"She rode away with her lover, became someone new, but I never forgot. Or forgave. I *never* stopped." He took a step toward them. "She wasn't safe here. I snuck in, I got to her…the same way I got to you." That hard laughter came again. "I know this land damn better than you all do. I spent so long watching, waiting, thinking I'd find what I'd lost."

No wonder the guy had been able to sneak onto the property. He'd probably mapped out the whole area long ago.

"She wouldn't tell me. Your father...*he wouldn't tell me.*"

"What do you want to know?" Sullivan rasped. "What was worth killing them for?"

"Family!" And it was a roar. A scream that cut through the night. "I wanted *my* family! Your father hid them from me. Took them...and I wanted them back!"

"Witness Protection," Celia cried out from behind Sullivan. "That's what this is about—they were hidden..."

"And I wanted them back!" His yell. "My woman. *My* child. But I didn't get them...and guess what? You won't get your family, either..."

He was squeezing the trigger. But Sullivan could hear the pounding of horses' hooves. He knew his family was coming. *I've always got them.*

Sullivan grabbed Celia and they flew toward the shelter of the nearest tree as gunfire erupted.

Gunfire from the shooter's weapon.

And gunfire...

"No one hurts my family," Davis snarled.

Gunfire from Davis's weapon.

Sullivan looked up. Davis still had his gun aimed at the masked man.

The shooter was on the ground.

Sullivan's shoulder throbbed and burned. He knew the masked man's bullet had hit him, but he didn't care about the wound. He was alive. Celia was alive. His family—*we're safe.*

"Sullivan?" Celia's fingers slid over his cheek.

His precious Celia.

"You're bleeding," she whispered.

So was she. They'd both earned new wounds from this night.

Davis jumped off his horse and closed in on the killer—on the man who'd taken so much from them. But he would *not* take any more.

"Doesn't even hurt," Sullivan said to her. He rose, pulling her with him, and he kept his arm around her.

Brodie had leaped off his horse, too, and Sullivan saw that Jennifer had already grabbed the shooter's weapon. She held it aimed at the prone man, her body tense.

"It's over," Sullivan said. "You're not hurting us anymore."

The fallen man just laughed. He rolled over, still wearing that mask. "The house is going to blow next," he said. "I've planted my bombs—you'll lose everything. All gone…in a puff of smoke."

Was he bluffing?

But…it didn't matter. "I'll lose nothing," Sullivan said. Blood dripped down his left arm. "Bricks and wood. The home will be rebuilt." It was the people who mattered.

Brodie leaned forward and ripped the mask off the guy's face.

Sullivan and Celia crept closer. Sullivan expected to see a stranger staring back at him.

He didn't.

He heard Celia's sharply indrawn breath.

The man's face was older, sharper, but…Sullivan had seen him before. In a very old photograph.

A photograph of his mother's brother.

No, no way…he wouldn't kill his own sister!

"I told her not to go…to the cops…" he rasped.

"When I shot that boy…I told her…I *warned* her, but she turned on me. *Me*."

A dull ringing filled Sullivan's ears. He stared at that man—*family*—and he'd never wanted to kill anyone more.

"Thought when Celia started digging…" The guy swiped his hand over his face and then his hand dropped to the ground beside him. "Thought she'd find out… that *I* was the one my sister identified all those years ago…that I was the one she ran from…"

A killer, intimately close.

Too close.

"Faked my death…Uncle Sam helped…I was killing for him…" He laughed. And his hand…it was sliding toward his boot. Sullivan's eyes narrowed.

"But then I learned what McGuire had done, what he'd taken…not just my sister…*everything*!" And his hand slid into his boot. Sullivan knew he was going to pull up a weapon, a gun or a knife, and Sullivan yelled a warning—

But Davis didn't need a warning. Davis didn't even need to fire. Neither did Jennifer. Because Monroe had managed to drag himself up. And Monroe took aim at the killer. The bullet blasted from Monroe's gun before anyone else could even move.

One bullet.

The killer fell back—*their uncle*. He tumbled into the dirt. His breath rasped out in a sick, rough gurgle, and Sullivan knew the bullet had found its mark. That was the last gasp of a dying man.

He bent next to the fallen man. The guy's eyes were still open—wide, desperate, a dark gold. A gold that Sullivan had seen before. Now he knew why Celia had gasped. She'd never seen the picture of his uncle. She hadn't recognized the guy from a photograph. She'd recognized his distinctive eyes.

Him.

When Sullivan had asked Alexandra to identify the shooter, she'd just said that the guy looked like…
"Him."

At the time, Sullivan had thought that the man must somehow look like him. But despite their blood connection, his uncle didn't resemble Sullivan at all.

Instead, his golden eyes looked exactly like Monroe Blake's. Exactly like the man who'd just killed him.

The golden eyes closed.

No one moved. Everyone stood there, staring at the dead man.

Past and present merged.

Grief twisted through Sullivan as he thought of all he'd lost.

Then…

Celia slipped closer. Her hand curled around his. "It's going to be okay," she said softly. "I promise. Everything will be okay…"

His fingers squeezed hers. The threat was finally over. Finally.

Sirens screamed in the distance.

Justice had come to the McGuire ranch.

Epilogue

The fires were out. The body was gone.

There were no more bombs. No more shooters lurking in the woods.

The ghosts from the past were gone.

There was just…family. And that family had gathered together at McGuire Securities, a somber meeting as they closed this final chapter.

Sullivan sat on the couch, his hands entwined with Celia's. They'd both been taken to the hospital. Patched up. Stitched. Released.

The cops had been there, interviewing them, asking questions that never seemed to end. Then the government had taken over. Agents in their fancy suits who were interested in containing the story.

After all, there were some secrets that weren't supposed to be shared.

Like the fact that their uncle—he'd been a trained assassin for the government. He'd spent years working with Ronald Worth, being the guy's attack dog. When Ronald needed a target eliminated, their uncle had been the man he called for the job.

After quite a few closed-door meetings with the CIA agents who'd swooped in, Celia had come to Sullivan to share what she'd learned. Apparently, Ronald had kept a secret file in his home office—a file that detailed all of their uncle's assignments for him. Once the powers that be at the agency had learned of his deception, Ronald's home was turned upside down. And all his secrets had been discovered.

Along with the truth about dear old Uncle Jeremiah.

Sullivan's mother had only mentioned him a few times. Her older brother. The soldier who'd survived battle but wound up dead at home. Sullivan had seen a picture of him, once. *Jeremiah.* He'd had dark hair and a wide smile.

Celia cleared her throat. "My contacts in the government have said that there will be no further inquiries on this investigation. As far as they're concerned, the case is closed."

The case. The McGuire legacy of pain and death. Now—over.

"He was a killer," Grant said, pushing back his shoulders. His voice was grim. "But he was her *brother.* Mom's own brother...he pulled the trigger."

Sullivan's gaze slid to his sister, Ava. He could never imagine hurting her. Would *never* do anything to so much as mar her skin. Tears glistened in Ava's eyes, and he hated that sight.

Davis was beside their sister. Ava's husband was to her right. Mark kept tenderly rubbing her shoulder.

"Every family has secrets," Celia said quietly, "and yours is certainly no exception."

No, theirs was the extreme.

"Your father...he helped your mother in many ways. It seems that she needed to make someone else disappear. Someone else that she feared Jeremiah might hurt.

It was never official. From what I've been able to learn, there was no record of this woman entering the Witness Protection Program."

All eyes were on her.

"Susan Salenger," she said quietly. "She was Jeremiah's lover over thirty years ago. His lover and your mother's best friend. When your mother saw what her brother had done, what he'd become, she knew that she had to get away from Jeremiah. She also knew that she had to protect her friend."

"But—but I thought Mom's brother was *dead*." Ava shook her head. "He was killed in a car accident. That was the story—"

"I'm afraid that's all it was. A story." Celia's voice was gentle. "Your uncle Jeremiah was working with Ronald. When it looked as though Jeremiah would be exposed, Ronald stepped in and tried to cover for the guy. After all, who looks for a dead man?"

Ava shivered.

"Ronald got rid of your mother's most damning evidence and Jeremiah…he got rid of the cops who'd heard her testimony. He ordered the hit on Henry, and then he made sure no one would connect the dots back to him…or Jeremiah."

Grant swore. "The guy was a damn monster."

Yes, he had been.

"Maybe your mother never bought the story of his death," Celia continued. "After all, she faked her own death, too, so maybe she suspected he was still out there all along."

"One death for another…" Grant shook his head. "And I never knew. She hid this all from us behind a wide smile."

Sullivan would never forget his mother's beautiful smile.

Silence lingered in the room until Ava said, "Jeremiah finally tracked down our mother, with Ronald's help."

Celia's voice was so quiet. "He wanted information from her. Or rather, from your father."

"He said…our dad said he'd never tell…" Ava's voice broke a bit.

"And he never did," Sullivan said.

"No." Celia shook her head. "He didn't. He never revealed what had become of Susan Salenger. He never told Jeremiah where she'd been taken. Who she'd become."

Grant surged to his feet. "Why the hell did she matter so much? Matter enough that Jeremiah killed his own sister?"

"She mattered…" Celia glanced at Sullivan, then continued. "Because she was pregnant. Ronald kept a file on Jeremiah, and in it he'd written that Jeremiah spent years looking for his child. Before Susan vanished, she was eight months pregnant. She had a baby, and Jeremiah wanted his son."

"Hell." Grant raked a hand over his face. "It was all about family."

In Jeremiah's twisted world, it had been. "I think the bastard wanted to punish Mom for betraying him—both for going to the cops after he told her to keep quiet, and then for taking Susan away…"

"Susan." Ava glanced around the room. Then her gaze focused on Celia. "Do we know what happened to her? What happened to her baby?"

There was a faint knock at the door.

Sullivan glanced at his watch. *Just in time.*

The door opened. Monroe Blake stood there. The faint lines near his eyes had deepened and the man appeared far too pale. He'd been in the hospital, but Sullivan knew he'd fought to get out early.

From all accounts, Monroe had always been a fighter.

"Sorry," Monroe said as he looked around. His golden eyes were wary. "I got a call from Celia telling me to be here."

Because Sullivan had asked her to make that call.

"Come in," Sullivan said. "You're just in time."

But Monroe didn't move. "No," he said. "I don't belong here. I just—I came to say how sorry I am. I came to say—"

"You didn't know he was your father," Sullivan interrupted. "Not until it was too late."

If possible, Monroe became even paler. "I'm nothing like him," he rasped.

Sullivan nodded. "No, I don't think you are."

Monroe stared at them all, his eyes tortured.

Celia had already told Sullivan what had happened to Susan. She'd become Katie Blake, and she'd given birth to a son.

Monroe.

A man who'd grown up and become a SEAL. A man who had—because fate was twisted and mysterious—saved Davis McGuire's life in battle, just as he, in turn, had been saved.

A man who was family, even though he hadn't realized it.

"I don't belong here," Monroe said. Shame flashed on his face.

Sullivan rose and went to his side. "Yes, you do."

And it was time they all let go of the pain from the past. It was time the McGuires looked to the future.

To hope.

"Welcome to the family…"

CELIA'S STOMACH WAS in knots. She'd been given the all clear from the agency. No one was coming after her—there were no more secrets she had to keep. She was…free.

Sullivan and his family were making peace with the past, and they were fully embracing Monroe. Poor, shell-shocked Monroe. The guy had killed his own father in order to save Sullivan.

She owed him. They all owed Monroe. She was sure the debt would be repaid.

They were back at the ranch. At the bluff that overlooked the lake. The water was still, and it reflected the sun, throwing the bright light back at her. But she didn't mind that light. After being in the darkness for so long, she found it nice.

"Are you hiding?"

She didn't tense at Sullivan's voice. After all, she'd known that he was coming. Deep inside, she'd always known they'd come together again.

Known. Hoped. Same thing.

She turned her head and found his gaze on her. Celia smiled at him. She barely even felt the pull of her stitches. Her new scar was nothing compared to what she could have lost.

Sullivan. And every hope she'd ever had.

"Not hiding," she said. "Just enjoying the sunset."

He reached for her hand. He was so warm and strong. And he was—

Kneeling.

"Sully?"

He had a ring in his fingers. "Will you marry me?"

"We...I...I think we are married." That part of Ronald's story had proven true. She just hadn't been able to tell Sully sooner because of—

He smiled up at her. "Then will you promise me forever, Celia? Because that's what I want. Forever, with you."

She couldn't speak.

His smile dimmed. "I've made mistakes. I know I've made so many, baby, but I swear, *you* are my world. I will do anything and everything to make you happy, I will—"

"I love you," Celia said.

His eyes darkened.

"And you've always had my forever." He'd had every part of her.

He slid the ring onto her finger. It was a perfect fit, and the diamond gleamed in the light. "You've always had my heart," he said gruffly. His fingers curled around hers. "Right here, it's been in the palm of your hand all along. You own me, Celia. Body and soul, and there is nothing I would not do for you."

Her own heart was pounding far too fast.

"I will love you forever," he promised her.

And she knew it was true. She could see that love on his face, in his eyes. And when he kissed her...she could feel it.

Forever.

The past was over, and their future waited.

* * * * *

INTRIGUE

Available May 24, 2016

#1641 WARRIOR SON
The Heroes of Horseshoe Creek • by Rita Herron
Deputy Sheriff Roan Whitefeather has been trying to avoid medical examiner Megan Lail since the night they spent together. But when the Horseshoe Creek ranch patriarch dies they will have to work together to investigate a web of murder and deception.

#1642 APB: BABY
The Precinct: Bachelors in Blue • by Julie Miller
Social worker Lucy McKane will do whatever it takes to protect the infant boy entrusted to her care. The sexy ME next door may be clueless about her feelings for him, but Niall Watson's the only one who can keep them safe.

#1643 ARMORED ATTRACTION
Omega Sector: Critical Response • by Janie Crouch
As Omega Sector agent Liam Goetz and his ex-fiancée Vanessa Epperson work together to save hostages and catch a predator, Liam begins to learn some shocking truths—about himself and the woman he thought he once knew so well...

#1644 DEEP SECRETS
Return to Ravesville • by Beverly Long
Rafe Roper "died" to protect his wife, Trish, from the criminals he was pursuing. But when Trish's life is put on the line, Rafe has no choice but to expose his lie and hope they don't both wind up dead—for real.

#1645 COLORADO CRIME SCENE
The Men of Search Team Seven • by Cindi Myers
With a ticking clock, undercover agent Luke Renfro must focus on his assignment in order to protect Morgan Westfield—the sister of the criminal he is chasing—and have any chance of seeing more of the woman he's falling for.

#1646 NATIVE BORN
Apache Protectors • by Jenna Kernan
Apache tribal council member Clyne Cosen needs the FBI's protection. But his custody battle with his personal bodyguard, Agent Cassidy Walker, muddles the line between personal and professional...

———————

YOU CAN FIND MORE INFORMATION ON UPCOMING HARLEQUIN® TITLES, FREE EXCERPTS AND MORE AT WWW.HARLEQUIN.COM.

HICNM0516

Her gaze darted up to meet his, and he felt her skin warming
beneath his touch before she turned her hand to squeeze
his fingers. Then she pulled away to finish packing. "But
we've already been too much of an imposition. You need
to go by St. Luke's to visit your grandfather and spend
time with your family. I've already kept you from them
longer than you planned this morning. I can grab the car
seat and call a cab so you don't even have to drive us.
Tommy and I will be fine—as long as you don't mind us
staying in your apartment. Maintenance said there was a
chance they could get someone to see to my locks today."

"And they also said it could be Monday morning." No.
Tommy needed Dr. Niall Watson of the KCPD Crime Lab
to be his friend right now. And no matter how independent
she claimed to be, Lucy needed a friend, too. Right now
that friend was going to be him. Niall shrugged into
his black KCPD jacket and picked up the sweater coat

she'd draped over the back of her chair. "I work quickly and methodically, Lucy. I will find the answers you and Tommy need. But I can't do that when I'm not able to focus. And having half the city between you and me when we don't know what all this means or if you and Tommy are in any kind of danger—"

"Are you saying I'm a distraction?"

Nothing but. Confused about whether that was some type of flirtatious remark or whether she was simply seeking clarification, Niall chose not to answer. Instead, he handed her the sweater and picked up Tommy in his carrier. "Get his things and let's go."

Don't miss APB: BABY
by USA TODAY *bestselling author Julie Miller,*
available June 2016 wherever
Harlequin® Intrigue books and ebooks are sold.

www.Harlequin.com

Reading Has Its Rewards

Earn **FREE BOOKS!**

Register at **Harlequin My Rewards** and submit your Harlequin purchases from wherever you shop to earn points for free books and other exclusive rewards.

Plus submit your purchases from now till May 30th for a chance to win a $500 Visa Card*.

Visit **HarlequinMyRewards.com** today

MYR16R1

THE WORLD IS BETTER WITH
Romance

Harlequin has everything from contemporary, passionate and heartwarming to suspenseful and inspirational stories.

Whatever your mood, we have a romance just for you!

Connect with us to find your next great read, special offers and more.

f /HarlequinBooks

🐦 @HarlequinBooks

www.HarlequinBlog.com

www.Harlequin.com/Newsletters

 HARLEQUIN®

A *Romance* FOR EVERY MOOD™

www.Harlequin.com